DATE DUE

JOCKIN THE JESTER

JOCKIN THE JESTER

by

Ursula Moray Williams

THOMAS NELSON INC.
Nashville • Camden • New York

Copyright © 1951, 1973 by Ursula Moray Williams

First U.S. edition

All rights reserved under International and Pan-American Conventions. Published by Thomas Nelson Inc., Nashville, Tennessee.

Library of Congress Cataloging in Publication Data

Williams, Ursula Moray.
  Jockin the Jester.
  SUMMARY: The adventures of a young jester during a peasant revolt in medieval England.
  [1. Great Britain—History—Medieval period, 1066–1485—Fiction. 2. Fools and jesters—Fiction]
  I. Title.
PZ7.W6683Jn3   [Fic]   72–14324
ISBN 0–8407–6276–3

To
BARBARA ARNASON

CONTENTS

Chapter 1

Birth of a Jester

One spring morning more than six hundred years ago, a happy peasant walked through the forest to his work.

His work was hard and his life was hard. He lived in a wooden hut thatched with straw and twigs, which let in the rain more often than was comfortable, because there never seemed time to mend it. His food was poor and his clothes were in rags, while more often than not he was too tired to be glad or sorry. Then the days passed wearily by. Work for the lord of the manor, work on his own strips of land and his neighbors', work gathering wood, work drawing water, through wet days and fine days, warm weather and cold weather, expecting nothing better, hoping for nothing worse; glad of a roof and a bed, a bowl of porridge, and a wife who did not scold too much—a man's life, a dull life, but after all, he wasn't born a lord, and there were many worse off than he with a cottage full of children to be fed and clothed.

Ah! But children brought happiness with them, and today he was a happy man because his first child lay in the wooden cradle—a son, the most beautiful child a man had ever had! A son to trot at his heels, to grow up, up, past his shoulders, past his ears, to carry water, chop wood, and push the plow along the warm brown furrows.

Could such a small red tender thing really become a man? Alas! thought the peasant, his heart sinking for a moment, what can manhood bring him? Work for the lord of the manor, work on his own strips of land and his neighbors', work gathering wood, work drawing water, through wet days and fine days, warm weather and cold weather, expecting nothing better, hoping for nothing worse; glad of a roof and a bed, a bowl of porridge, and maybe a wife of his own by and by—that's all a man's life is—a dull life, but after all, we aren't all born lords.

No, but we aren't all born laughing, as the wise woman had said when she took the baby from his mother and laid him in his rough wooden cradle. She swore the child had smiled at his birth, but when the father looked at him he lay there as solemn as a little owl, and perhaps the wise woman was only trying to please the new mother.

How she had rattled on as she warmed the brew of herbs she had brought with her and held it to the peasant woman's lips. "Such a beautiful boy! And born smiling, when everyone knows all babies cry first at seeing the light! He will not be hard to please! He will be a laughter maker. You had better make a jester of him!"

The mother's eyes had brightened when she heard these words, thinking: everyone knows that a jester has a good position in a noble house, good food, good clothes, and a certain consequence. He follows his lord everywhere, and if someday he is exchanged or given away, it is always to a house of equal dignity. And if a jester should happen to please a king, his fortune is made. His position becomes almost royal. The mother had closed her eyes, dreaming of her son as court jester.

But the father paid no heed to the wise woman's words, till deep in the forest he met his lord a-hunting. The lord of the manor owned many acres of the forest and surrounding land, some of which was cultivated by his peasants.

In payment for his work, each peasant owned a few

strips of the same land, which he plowed for his own use. Jockin, the peasant father, being of no particular importance, owned a few strips close to a ditch. Weeds filled the ditch, and in the summer their seeds blew over Jockin's land, so he always had hard work to clear it and keep up with his neighbors. But he took it as his lot, and before long, there would be a son hoeing beside him. Two men could keep down the weeds and soon clear the ditch.

Thinking in this way, poor Jockin was so busy dreaming of the *chep-chep-tek!* of the hoe and the imaginary prattle of his son that he did not hear the baying of hounds and the shouting of huntsmen before a large boar broke cover in front of him and crossed the path into an opposite thicket.

Hounds and huntsmen followed in noisy confusion; the whole bright picture passed Jockin's vision and disappeared before his slow peasant brain could assimilate it. He stayed openmouthed in the center of the path, slowly swinging his wooden hoe, the smile that had never left his face all the morning still transfixed, although his mouth was open and his eyes were goggling.

He was almost overridden by a party of riders galloping up the path behind him.

Jockin was accustomed to being cursed at by his betters. After all, if a man lives in a noble house he has more right to the space he takes up on the earth than a poor peasant. And if a poor peasant gets in the way, he must expect to be knocked down. So Jockin considered himself lucky as he scrambled out of the way unharmed and listened to the stream of curses poured on his head by the young lord of the manor.

The curses were echoed word for word by an ugly little dwarf riding a pony behind his master. When at last the torrent of abuse was exhausted, the dwarf continued to babble, "Look at him now! Grinning like an ape! Grinning like an ape! Grinning like an ape!" as if he were wound up and did not know how to stop himself.

"Be quiet!" his lord angrily shouted at him. Then, turning to Jockin, he added curiously, "And what have you got to grin about, I'd like to know?"

Jockin now became aware of the rest of the party. In all, four figures on horses and ponies were lined up on the path, staring at him sprawled there on the bank.

Beside his own young lord a strange nobleman was quietly watching the scene, while behind him a jester in motley, with bells on cap and sleeves, secretly teased his white pony into crazy antics that threatened to tumble them both into the bushes.

The smile that all day had never left Jockin's face since first he beheld his small red son in the wooden cradle, now broadened at the sight of the jester.

"Come! what are you grinning about, man?" his lord repeated, more impatient than curious.

Jockin pointed clumsily at the jester and, raising himself on his elbow, muttered hoarsely, "Today I became father of a son such as he is!"

The jester pretended to swoon with surprise, then, tumbling off his pony at the peasant's feet, advanced upon him with open arms, crying, "Father! Father! My aged parent! Long lost! Long wept for!" with such comical gestures that the two noblemen rocked with merriment. "Or am I mistaken?" continued the jester, recoiling in mock dismay at the peasant's rebuff. "Was it he at whom you pointed?" And he indicated the dwarf. "Ah then, my poor friend, you are much to be pitied, for such as these are born at their greatest, and become of less account every year until they go about unnoticed, being of no size at all!"

Again the noblemen laughed, this time at the dwarf, who flashed a spiteful glance at his tormentor, knowing very well that he was losing popularity in his lord's house through laziness and greed. Besides, like most small people, he could not bear to be mocked or laughed at.

"Which is it?" the strange nobleman asked. "Have you fathered a clown or a monkey this bright morning? Whichever it is, here's a penny for him!" And he threw down a coin.

"And here's another!" added the young lord of the manor, tossing a second coin to Jockin.

"And another!" cried the jester, pulling off one of his bells. "Believe me, good money should always ring when you sound it, and a good ring of money will always bring you friends, poor fellow! So tell your son to ring his money truly, and as money runs to money, he'll maybe make a fortune. Just listen to the ringing!" And he tossed the bell into Jockin's lap.

"Now, Dobbin—pay your share!" the incorrigible jester added, turning on the dwarf. "Your pockets must be heavy with gold to keep you so close to the earth. Out with your riches and watch yourself grow up in the night!"

But the dwarf angrily wrenched a loose button from his cloak and flung it on the ground without a word.

"Oho!" said the jester, "A bone button is a poor present to give. Maybe the babe will swallow it!"

"I hope he will!" said the spiteful dwarf, backing the pony to sulk behind his lord.

"Thank you, my lords and good masters!" stammered the peasant, awkwardly fumbling in the leaves for his treasures. Then with a tremendous effort, he added, "And when my son is of an age, my lord, you may have him, if you will, to entertain you!"

The two noblemen laughed heartily as they spurred their horses to follow the hunt.

"I'll be needing a new ape to take the place of this one!" said the younger, with a contemptuous gesture at the dwarf. "Don't forget your bargain, moonface! And don't get yourself trampled to death again before you've brought up your boy to be my fool!"

They cantered away, the jester making absurd imitations of rocking a baby to sleep in his arms as he weaved his pony to and fro to jostle the dwarf and amuse his masters.

The two noblemen thought no more of the incident, but to Jockin it was a serious occasion that became of greater importance the longer he pondered over it. By the time he had worked all day on his lord's land, the careless words flung backward to him had become a promise ensuring the future success of his baby son.

Uneducated and unused to thinking, he pondered so heavily all the way home that he arrived in a state of stupor. The wise woman had gone, leaving a brew to be given to the mother that Jockin clumsily heated and brought her in a wooden cup. As he bent over his wife she heard the clink of coins in the bag he carried at his belt, such an unusual sound in that poor home that she started, spilling the brew, and asked, "Whatever have you there?"

Jockin did not intend to keep anything from her, but the weight and importance of his adventure were still so heavy upon him that he could not yet put it into words. All he could say, after a considerable pause, was, "My lord of the manor gave me a penny for our child and another nobleman gave me a second."

The mother looked from her husband to her son as if such wonderful fortune were beyond understanding. The baby lay snugly in her arms; once again it seemed to be almost smiling.

"The wise woman told us of happiness for him!" she murmured. "And riches must bring happiness, since what is there for a poor man on this earth but hunger and cold and toil? Did they say anything else to you?" she asked her husband.

The peasant shook his head, feeling quite unable to describe the scene further that evening. But later in the night he woke his sleeping wife to mutter hoarsely, "He says I have to bring up the boy to be his jester!"

So the wise woman was right! thought the wondering mother, and she imagined her child the pet of a noble house, in motley, with cap and bells.

Chapter 2

Jockin the Jester

The Black Death swept through medieval England in 1348, fifteen years after little Jockin, son of Plow Jockin the peasant, was born.

For several years now the two had worked side by side on their lord's land, and on their own narrow strips, which provided them with just enough to keep them fed and clothed. Plow Jockin was no genius; mechanically he gave of his best toil, and mechanically took what return was offered him. His few strips of land never became many, though some of his neighbors doubled and then trebled their property and were looked on as rich men. Some men bought their freedom from the manor and worked as they pleased and for whom they pleased, disappearing at times for months on end and returning to their homes with finery and possessions and tales of town life and opportunity that astonished and disturbed the simple peasants, who could hardly conceive of such wide experience.

No other children had come. Jockin's mother fed her pigs and poultry and sat at her spinning wheel uncluttered by a crowd of little ones. But she thought herself the poorer for it, and sighed for her old age and her son's future. Several brothers could work together and enrich themselves, but what could one alone hope for himself, with the whole world waiting to do him down? That was the poor woman's experience of her neighbors, and she secretly blamed her husband for it, just as she blamed him for everything else, the thistles on his land, the way

16

the snow came through the roof in winter, and the blight on the cabbages.

And when, occasionally, she remembered the words of the wise woman and the story Plow Jockin had brought home the day of little Jo's birth, she blamed her husband, too, for the failure of all their plans and hopes. Little Jo seldom smiled now. He had grown into a tall, thin, serious child. Even had he become a dwarf (and she had the whole story from Plow Jockin by degrees), he would have had a better chance to please their lord and master than this pale, lanky youth, old before his time from work and privation. Still she regularly asked his father the same question:

"When are you going to take our Jo to the manor house?"

And Plow Jockin always answered with the same words:

"As he grows older his wits will sharpen, and when they are sharp enough I will take him."

But there was little sign of any sharpness in Jockin the Younger's wits. He appeared as slow as his father, as honest and as easygoing. Even his mother could not see a brilliant future for this beloved only child, and as for the wise woman, there was no reason for her to come to the cottage anymore, so she stayed away.

Years ago, Plow Jockin's wife had bought two strips of bright material, one red, one yellow, from a traveling merchant and sewed them into a little pointed cap. At the point she sewed the bell the jester had tossed to Plow Jockin, and fastened it with the dwarf's button. With the two coins she had bought a length of yellow cloth and made it into a suit for her son with dyed-red stockings and a plaited belt. She made it secretly, while the little boy followed his father, tilling the land.

When he came home she dressed him in this finery,

and gazing at the solemn little face under the cap and bell, she said to him, "Now you must learn to sing and dance and make merry, because lords like to be amused from morning till night. Let me see you do it!" At that time she felt sure her child could entertain a world of kings, were he put in a position to do so.

But little Jo only smiled at her with the wide, sweet, sudden smile he kept for no one else, standing awkwardly on the mud floor, with the reed, which she had given him for a bauble, dangling on his toes, saying nothing, doing nothing. However, the smile soon vanished.

"Dance a caper!" she ordered him. Little Jo capered awkwardly like a calf.

"Sing and laugh!" his mother shouted. When he could do neither, she burst into tears.

"Can't you even smile?" she scolded, boxing his ears.

The little boy dropped his reed and sobbed. They were both crying when Plow Jockin came in, gaping at their tears.

When he heard the reason he was very angry.

"Can't you leave well enough alone, foolish woman?" he shouted. "The lord doesn't want a baby at his table! All will come in its own good time. Here is good money spent on a suit that is no good to anybody, since it will be too small for our boy when he goes to the manor, and who else is going to buy a suit of red and yellow?"

The wife put away the suit and for months did not dare to mention Jockin's future. Plow Jockin, of course, did not share her fears. Things were working out no better and no worse than he had expected.

His son worked by his side, the ditch was cleared out, the weeds were destroyed. If he did not become rich like his neighbors, at least he was comfortable, and by and by he would take his boy to the manor just as he had promised his lord. Only not just yet. The jester Plow Jockin remembered had been tall and manly, even a better figure than his master. Looking at little Jo, the father remembered the dwarf—how he had been teased and laughed at. His son was not a dwarf, but let him grow tall and straight, so nobody dared ever to mock him. He was only a child and needed his mother's care, even needed her scolding and her reproaches, just as Plow Jockin had needed them himself.

Then the Black Death came. Over the peasants in their humble homes it rode like a robber, wresting from them the hardly won comfort for which they had struggled, and which their parents and grandparents had never known. Their fields lay masterless, and were reclaimed by the lords who had sold them. Their pigs and cows starved, died, ran wild, or were appropriated. Labor became scarce, and the peasants asked high wages of their lords who had used them so cheaply.

Little Jo lay sweating with the terrible sickness in his parents' cottage and saw again through fever-distorted eyes the wise woman who had attended his birth. The terrified mother could do nothing but wring her hands and hamper the wise woman with her fear and wretchedness.

"All we had expected for him!" sobbed the poor woman. "All the promises made him! All you prophesied for him! All unfulfilled."

"Nonsense!" said the wise woman, elbowing the mother aside as she bent over the sick boy and caught the first sign of unexpected improvement in his face. "Look!" she said, pointing. "The boy is smiling again and will certainly recover. Only a jester laughs at death."

And little Jo recovered, to his parents' pride and joy, though his smile had been only the fragment of a feverish dream, but they felt the wise woman knew all his future, and this second prophecy must not be ignored.

Next time his mother said to Plow Jockin (weeks later, when little Jo was walking around, paler, taller, and more serious than ever), "When are you going to take our Jo to the manor?" Plow Jockin replied, "I shall take him tomorrow."

That evening his mother brought out the yellow suit and the red-and-yellow cap with the bell on it. She knitted an extra band around the tops of the scarlet stockings, but even so, when little Jo put them on in the morning, they were pitifully short, and the sleeves of the suit came halfway up his arms. The cap, too, sat oddly on the top of his head. Little Jo wrenched off the dwarf's button trying to fasten it under his chin. The only part of the suit that fitted was the breadth of it, for the poor boy was terribly thin since his fever, and so tall and gaunt that many would have taken him for a man. Plow Jockin said nothing when he saw the suit and the ridiculous cap and bell. He felt sure the time had come to keep his bargain with the lord of the manor. The terrible illness must have been sent as a sign to remind him he must no longer cling to his son.

Together they set off through the forest, while the mother stayed behind spinning hopes into her thread, and picturing her son in the splendid position that awaited him in the manor house.

Plow Jockin lived some way from the village and the manor house. His parents had been wanderers who had built the cottage on an outlying part of the lord's land, and had fed their beasts there till they slowly came under the lord's tenancy, with its accompanying duties and privileges. Plow Jockin had inherited their independence, and although he worked for his lord, he never tried to better his surroundings nor move nearer his neighbors in the village.

He had not seemed to notice the prosperity that had slowly raised the standard of living of the farm laborer and manor tenant, but his wife knew what she was missing and resented it bitterly. However, their isolation may have helped to stave off the Black Death, for few vanquished it as little Jo had done. His parents escaped the sickness completely, but in the village, half the population died within a few weeks.

Little Jo, who was no longer little but only young, kept his eyes downcast as they passed down the village street. He heard and felt the ridicule of the women and children at his peculiar clothes. Their jeering was the more spiteful because the wise woman had manged to save his life while most of their own children had died.

Plow Jockin took the laughter hopefully and decided his wife had been right. Young Jo's motley and bells amused people; he would certainly be successful with his lord of the manor.

The way was not new to either of them. To the village people the manor kitchen was the center of their life; it was their marketplace and gossip bench. Thence they carried their produce, their eggs, lambs, poultry, and cloth. There they dallied many pleasant hours, while the manor life busied around them and saucy pages ran in on errands, sticking their fingers into juicy pies and cheeking the cooks.

Plow Jockin had come too, less often, and brought young Jo carrying his mother's eggs or yarn. The hubbub and jostling dazed the boy; he was always thankful to turn his back on the manor and tramp home again through the forest. Yet the manor kitchen had a strange fascination for him, and after it the cottage seemed lonely.

He had a great love for people, so deep and natural that the greatest wit could not have persuaded him to make fun of anyone in malice. It was not in his nature. He could not see that human failings were funny, or laugh when the cook upset boiling fat on the foot of a fat serving maid, so that she leaped four feet onto a bench, squawking. He hated to see the pages tie the cats' tails together, or even to hear them imitate the lady of the manor scolding her husband. And this tenderhearted, serious boy was walking to the manor house to become his lord's jester.

Chapter 3

The Daughter of the Manor

The eldest daughter of the manor house was crouching in the bracken, cherishing her last few precious moments of freedom before punishment came.

And how well deserved a punishment! Her heart, thumping wildly from her last glorious rush downhill, beat a little faster when she began to count her sins of the day, not in the quiet, sorrowful manner she counted them before and during confession, with kind Father Francis waiting with such infinite patience to help her make her peace with God, but with quick, anxious recollection and quicker heartbeats, as the awful list piled up and God seemed farther and farther away—her mother closer and closer.

If only her mother were more like God, that is, patient, understanding, forgiving, as Father Francis pictured Him to be. Mother wasn't patient. She had so much to see to, so much to do, so many people to find fault with, it had really become a habit. And she wasn't understanding, or she wouldn't be always preventing her daughters from enjoying themselves, and forcing them to sit for hours at horrible embroidery, or threatening to send them to convents. She wasn't forgiving—even after punishment she seldom appeared to pardon. Her daughters felt their sins pile up from one wickedness to another; with her they never started fresh and clean again, as after half an hour with God and Father Francis.

Mother was different with the boys. Edward, whom she

adored, was away serving as squire to his uncle in Wales. He was always understood, always forgiven. Mother had endless patience for him, and for Philip too—lucky Philip, taught by Father Francis and cherished by Mother. Such an easy, pleasant life!

Little Katherine seemed to find it easy to be good, she was so placid and sweet-tempered. She sometimes said she would like to go into a convent. Soft thing!

Barbara flung herself back on the springy grass, so that the great blue arch of sky was fringed by fronds and spears and tassels.

She knew she would be beaten and shut up in the nursery, with tiny Isabel and the gloomy old nurse, for days and days and days, and the dwarf, whom she hated, would bring their food. But oh, what a wonderful, beautiful, terrifying day she had had, and how nearly it was over!

Early in the morning she had stolen from the family's private rooms in the manor house into the hall and cut off her hair with her mother's embroidery scissors! The thick golden tresses were difficult to sever, and halfway through, when they lay strewn around her feet, she gazed helplessly at the attendants sleeping in the center of the hall on their rushes, hoping wildly that one of them would wake up and prevent her. But no one stirred. She cut and hacked till her head was shorn, then swept up the golden armful and fled through the dark stone passage into the kitchen, thrusting it into the ashes of the open fireplace. The betraying smell of singeing hair followed her back to her rooms, but long before little Katherine woke, Barbara was creeping on tiptoe to the pages' quarters, empty now save for one boy who had suffered from the Black Sickness and, being still frail and sickly, was excused from an early rising. After his companions had dressed and gone, the boy had fallen asleep again, and Barbara stole his clothes without difficulty.

Back in her own part of the house she dressed quickly behind an arras and ran down to join the other pages, as handsome a boy as any of them, save for the ends of her hair, which had been raggedly cut, particulary at the nape of her neck.

The boys were shocked, admiring, and apprehensive all at once. She was their playmate and good friend, though half of them were always on the wrong side of her hot temper and sharp tongue. Their welcome was hilarious, and the bursts of laughter filling the hall so early in the morning raised the suspicions of the short-sighted steward, who thought they were laughing at him and railed at them quite vainly from time to time. Oh, the glory of queening it in disguise!

By the time her absence was discovered, Barbara was in the yard with the rest of the pages and squires, tilting on horseback at a wooden figure that revolved if ill missed, giving its challenger a resounding blow as he galloped by. It was a sport Barbara had long watched and envied; not till a fierce knock laid her in the dust did she admit to herself that it might be an overrated pastime. Some of the Lady Isabel's attendants, watching from above, wondered why the other squires rushed to pick up their companion and examine his hurts, instead of roaring with laughter as they usually did at such an accident.

One of the squires had the boldness to kiss her on the cheek as he picked her up out of the dust. It was a boy Barbara particularly detested, and she gave him a rousing blow on the nose. He dropped her immediately, while the rest quickly hid the little scene from the view of the onlookers. But the angry squire immediately shook off his companions and, slipping away, went to find the steward, the chaplain, or any other person in authority who would help him avenge his humiliation.

The boys saw that the game was finished. So did Barbara. Before inquiries could be made, she was back in her rooms and in her own dress, with a wimple tied demurely around her hair. Wimples were out of fashion except as mourning, but her grandmother had lately died, and her mother looked quite approvingly when Barbara curtsied good morning.

Barbara followed the Lady Isabel into the kitchen, hoping the hot ashes had finally disposed of her hair. Passing through the hall she met the squire who had annoyed her, and his eyes became round with astonishment at beholding her dressed as usual. But something in her haughty and angry stare told him the truth. For the moment he let mother and daughter pass, bowing low to the lady of the manor, but a few moments later, when she stood fidgeting in the kitchen at her mother's side, Barbara saw him once more advancing, this time with a purposeful air. Feverishly she put a hand behind her and seized a pot of honey standing by in preparation for the bread that was to be made today. The squire saw nothing but her angry eyes as she placed herself between him and her mother. Still he did not waver but walked sternly on.

"My Lady Isabel . . ." he began.

Barbara whisked the pot of honey from behind her skirts and clapped it on his head. As the honey poured down his face onto his shoulders and handsome tunic, she gave him a kick on the shins that set him squawking, and fled from the kitchen.

The dwarf, who already knew the squire's story, attempted to stop her in the corridor.

"I hate you, you horrid little man!" Barbara cried, giving him a great push. He snatched angrily at her wimple, which fell off, exposing her ragged locks. A gasp of horror encircled the hall, but Barbara guessed she was still invisible to her mother in the kitchen. With her wimple in disarray and her shorn head tossing in fury, she escaped from the hall, ran through the courtyard, and at the outer wall climbed a pear tree, well proved by herself and Edward in happier days gone by.

The manor house had been built by Barbara's father. It was no longer bastioned and defended, as were the houses of a previous century. Barbara found no difficulty in climbing the outer wall and dropping onto the grass a stone's throw away from the village green. Her dress was torn in two places, and she had lost a shoe in climbing. With her rumpled head and wimple, smears of dust across her hot, excited face, and spoiled clothes, she did not look as good as some of the village girls, who were displaying bright gowns bought in the city.

The green was crowded, for some wandering entertainers had arrived with juggling balls and dancing bears. The house emptied as people surged around them. Among the crowd Barbara recognized many of the manor inhabitants, servants of her mother or of her father, and others who were accustomed to come almost daily to the kitchen. But she was not noticed. She stole gleefully from one knot of spectators to another, half regretful that she dared not go back and fetch little Katherine, half triumphant to be madcapping about the village on her own account.

Accustomed to commanding others, Barbara did not hesitate to use her elbows, and even her feet, to force her way to the front of the people, who grumbled at her and knocked her about, but gave way to her imperiousness. One or two recognized her, looking in vain for an attendant or even for her brother, and wondering at her

state of dress. But the clever actors took most of the attention, and nearly an hour was gone before Barbara,
with a sudden wary glance toward the manor house, beheld the dwarf emerging purposefully from the gate as
though on some important errand.

He has come to look for me! she thought at once.
Hastily she ran around the circle till the crowd stood
between her and the dwarf. Then, picking up her skirts,
away she ran across the green, dodging behind a cottage
and off into the forest where no one would be likely to
find her.

A day in her own company was such an unexpected
pleasure that Barbara did not at first trouble to think
of the consequences. No sewing. No singing practice. No
tiresome standing for hours beside her mother, busy with
household tasks. No minding of baby sister or quarreling
with Philip. No sermons from the chaplain. No sip of
wine from her father's cup—but at that thought Barbara's
face clouded. She dearly loved and admired her father,
envying his pages and squires, who accompanied him
wherever he went. The fear of being sent to a convent
was chiefly the dread of leaving him. His smile banished
her ill temper; it developed her dignity and better quali-
ties. His anger was her despair and loosed her tears. She
leaned against a tree, the morning spoiled.

Then she remembered her father was to leave the manor
at noon to view the distant part of his estate and would
not be back until late. Tomorrow was so far away, it was
not worth considering; she even had a wild fancy that her
hair might grow again. Cramming her mouth with de-
licious little wild strawberries, she roamed the woods,
picturing herself the lost princess of a fairy tale, such as
had been told her by her uncle's jester last Christmas.

She slaked her thirst at a forest stream, watching a hind

and a fawn drinking too, farther down. She made a wreath of leaves for her head, and slept long under a bush to make up for the lost sleep of the morning. And so at last the golden day ended in the golden peace of the woods, and crouching in the bracken, with the fronds waving gently over her head against a blue sky into which was creeping a tint of emerald and yellow—warning of sunset —Barbara felt the morning's events so far away, her life in the manor so distant, that she could hardly believe she was really part of it at all.

But return was inevitable. The woods were fearful at night. When darkness hid the strawberries and wild flowers, robbers, wild animals, and other dangers would begin to prowl. She did not want to linger after twilight, not though all the punishments in the world awaited her at home.

Suddenly she felt intensely lonely. It was all she could do not to cry out for her younger brother Philip. Even little Katherine or the warm body of baby Isabel would have been a comfort to her. She had seen nobody all day since she had left the village green. Now she felt as if nobody else existed. Suppose enemies had come to the manor, as in the days of her grandfather, and burned it to the ground! Suppose the Black Sickness had returned and everyone had perished! Suppose, because of her wickedness, the manor gates had been closed against her so she could not return!

The brambles clutched at the tattered remnants of Barbara's dress as she sprang up and struggled through the undergrowth. Once free of the little glade where she had been lying, she plunged into the shadowy woods, which grew darker every moment. She could not find any path. This morning she had delighted in making her own way from glade to glade, scorning the ways trodden by people whose business lay in the forest. And now when she looked wildly for them, no tracks were to be found.

Unused to being alone, bewildered at being thwarted, furious because there was nobody to scold or blame, Barbara burst into angry, hysterical tears. She beat her hands against the trees as though they would make way for her. It was no longer amusing to walk half barefoot. Where in daylight there had been soft moss, now in twilight were only stones, sharp sticks, and thorns. She began to cry louder than baby Isabel.

An old blind hermit lived not far away in a cave that for many years had been his home. Barbara's sobs reached his ears as he plodded homeward from a spring where he fetched his drinking water. He had not heard a child crying for many, many years, and his sight was too dim to find her among the trees.

"Where are you, my child, where are you?" he quavered. He spoke so seldom that his voice was high and cracked, but Barbara heard it. She saw his brown, ragged figure through the trees and ran stumbling toward him. He was so old, so dirty, and so venerable she felt sure he must be a hermit.

"Oh, Father!" she sobbed. "Please save me and tell me the way to my father's house! I'm so frightened and so tired and the woods are so terrible!"

"Poor child!" said the hermit, stroking her tousled head. "Are the woods really so full of terror for you? I find them full of God."

"Ah, but I've been so wicked!" Barbara sobbed. "You are a good, holy man, and you cannot know what I have suffered. Please tell me the way back to my father's manor, oh, please do! I shall beg pardon of God and of my mother and never be wicked again!"

"Why wait to ask forgiveness till you are safe?" the

hermit asked sternly. "If truly you are a daughter of the manor house, then gay living and prosperity will dim your memories all too soon. Now is the time to ask pardon."

"I will! I will!" Barbara cried, sinking to her knees. She bent her head while the hermit murmured a prayer. Suddenly she felt brave and strong again. She wished the good, holy, dirty old man would tell her the way and let her go. But his gnarled brown hand was on her shoulder.

"I cannot take you there," he said. "It is twenty years since I went a mile from my cave. I cannot even see the path you must follow, only the narrow little track I have worn in fetching water. But if you follow it, you will come to a spring. Cross the spring by the flat stone where people put out crusts and bones for me. Behind the stone you will see another, wider track. Follow this a long way till you come to a cottage. The people there are kind, they will take you home." He dropped his hand abruptly and shuffled away down the path.

Barbara had been on the point of kissing the ragged hem of his robe as she had been taught to do to visiting friars and pilgrims, but she was not sorry to be excused. She had never seen quite such a dirty old man in her life, though he was probably very good and very holy.

She ran down the track to the spring where, sure enough, a flat stone stood, and behind the stone she saw a wider, well-worn track through the forest.

Barbara felt sure it led away from her home, but if it took her to human company, she did not mind, for a little wind was fanning the tops of the trees after the fashion of early evening, and the sound was lonely and eerie.

As it grew darker and darker, she had to stop running

and feel her way. She bumped into the trunks of trees as the track turned and twisted; which foot was the most bruised and cut, she could no longer tell. Baby Isabel's cold turret nursery now seemed like a haven; she sobbed enviously, thinking of herself there. Even the dwarf became an angel.

Suddenly a black object, even darker than the darkness, loomed in front of her, too large for a tree—it was a hut! A faint gleam of light shone through the rough log walls, and Barbara's shout brought someone to the door bearing a rush candle. It was the wife of Plow Jockin, waiting for her man to come home and tell her of the great fortune awaiting her son at the manor.

She was so anxious for news of him she had forgotten to be afraid at hearing a strange voice outside the door in the evening.

If Barbara had thought the hermit dirty, Plow Jockin's wife was just as shocked to see the ragged, scratched, and tousled girl who stood before her.

Something in Barbara's voice and imperious manner told her she was of noble birth and position, but her appearance was more savage than that of the gypsies and vagrants who sometimes passed through the lord's forests on their restless journeys.

"Who lives here?" Barbara demanded, seeing that it was a poor house and the woman was more plainly dressed than any in the village or the manor.

"Plow Jockin, my lady," replied the wife, anxiously dropping a curtsy, as she wondered if this noble child had escaped from robbers or from the clutches of wild beasts.

"Is he within?" Barbara asked.

"No, my lady. He is far from home. He is gone to the manor house, but I expect him shortly."

"To the manor house? Why, that is my home!" exclaimed Barbara. "What does he want there? Is he gone to see our steward?"

"No, my lady. My lord has asked for our son to go as jester. Jockin, my husband, has taken him there."

"As *jester!*" Barbara's eyes sparkled with interest. She pushed her way into the rude cottage past the woman, grimacing at the smoke from the humble fire, at the rough walls and mud floor, but glad to fling herself down on a bench and stretch out her feet to the fire. "Tell me more of this," she commanded. "You say my lord has sent for your son to be his jester?"

Privately she was thinking it strange that she had heard nothing of this from her father or her mother. Accustomed to following her mother around with all the household tasks, and lately permitted to sit on her father's knee at supper, she heard most of their conversations, and this must have been discussed in the secret of their own rooms to escape her ears. She had always pleaded for her father to have a jester, such an amiable, pleasant, amusing fellow as her uncle brought with him when he came to visit them. But for some reason or other, the Lady Isabel could not tolerate them, and as she held great sway over her husband, the manor hall remained empty of cap and bells, and the dwarf, who had been part of Lady Isabel's dowry, reigned supreme.

Barbara began to regret she had not been at the manor house to welcome the new jester.

"This son of yours then—has he a good wit?"

"Oh, an excellent wit, your ladyship!" the mother assured her, convincing even herself now that her son was so far away and she so lonely for him.

"Does he tell a lively tale?" Barbara wanted to know.

"Indeed he does!" the mother promised, quite certain

that young Jo could do all anyone wished in this direction.

"Is he handsome?" the girl wanted to know, too young to realize that to a mother her son is always a prince among men.

"He looks like an angel, my lady," the poor woman said, "and in his cap and bells with his new yellow suit and red stockings, why, he's bound to please your ladyship, my lady!"

"I am impatient to see him!" said Barbara, feeling much refreshed by some milk and the warmth. "When may we be gone?"

"Why—in the darkness . . . in this peril of nighttime . . ." said the woman anxiously. "I doubt if I could find the way. I have never been to the manor house, and it is a long way from here. My husband knows every step of the road. Let us wait till he comes in!"

"Let's go and meet him!" said Barbara, who began to be aware of the smell of pigs behind the cottage, the smoke and mud within.

"We might miss him on the road, my lady!" the peasant woman protested. "And look at your poor feet! Let me bind them for you, or you will never walk all that way."

Barbara submitted with a good grace to having her feet bound up in rags, and even tried on a pair of the peasant's pattens to take the place of her remaining battered shoe. Then she stretched, yawned, and lay down uncomfortably the length of the bench. "I will have a nap till your husband returns," she said. "Put another log on the fire, my good woman, and rouse me when he comes."

Plow Jockin's wife sat beside the sleeping girl, her head full of bewilderment. What advancement was coming to the family, all in one day! Her son taking a position in the manor house and now the daughter of the manor seeking shelter at their fire. How she came to be in such a condition the peasant woman was not bold enough to ask, but surely her noble parents would not fail to reward the humble family that had protected and restored her. The mother weaved rosy dreams of her son, the poor jester, married to a noble lady like this lovely, bedraggled girl.

But why did such a beautiful child wear her hair so short and ragged? One would almost think it had been cut off.

The fire died down. Presently footsteps sounded outside.

Plow Jockin's wife looked up in surprise at hearing more than one pair of feet shuffling on the doorstep. Who could be with her husband? She went to open the door.

When the poor woman saw who had come home with Plow Jockin, tears of surprise and dismay filled her eyes. The last person in the world she had expected to see was young Jo, her son. Without a word she backed into the room before them, staring and staring from her husband to the boy. She had quite forgotten the girl asleep on the bench.

"Who is that, Mother?" young Jo asked, pointing at Barbara.

Still the mother could not speak.

Plow Jockin pushed past her to bend over the girl asleep. "Why, this is the young lady from the manor there's been such an uproar about!" he said curiously. "Did you ever see a lady in such a state? Did you cut her hair, good wife?"

"Not I!" said his wife indignantly. "Just as she lies now she came to me, all torn and draggled, with one shoe on and one shoe off and her hair full of bracken and brambles. What could I do but let her rest till you came home?"

Then, turning to her son, she added in a kind of wail, "And why are you come too?"

The boy hung his head. "My lord is not in need of a jester!" he mumbled.

At that moment Barbara awoke, and stared, as well she might, to see the small cottage full of people, including the tall youth in his odd homemade motley. She heard his last words and her eyes flashed indignantly.

"What? Has my lord changed his mind?" she demanded. "You told me he was asked for!" she added accusingly to the woman.

"He was! He was!" said the poor woman, sobbing. "Sixteen years ago the promise was made; isn't that true, Husband?"

Plow Jockin nodded gloomily; his reception at the manor house had embittered him toward his lord's family. True, they were distracted and out of their wits with worry over the disappearance of the eldest daughter of the house—but after they had waited long, long hours in the kitchen my lord had not returned, and my lady had driven them from the place, ridiculing his story, scoffing at his son, and shrieking at them both.

"Go back to the fields and work! That is where we want our servants! The plow and harrow lie idle since the Black Death! Who wants a jester? Take your quip and jest to the furrows, my good man, if you want to please your master!"

Plow Jockin, too slow and too proud to boast of the acres he had plowed and his son had hoed, got up without a word and left the distracted lady to her grief. He never even asked his son's opinion, but plodded slowly back through the forest to his home. And there he found the daughter of the manor in front of his own fire. An odd world, to be sure.

"A promise is a promise!" Barbara said. "Men fight for broken promises—fight to the death! Take me home, and you shall tell me the story of that promise on the way. I am sure my father will never fail you. Tell me, did you see him, or only our steward?"

"My lord was from home. The steward told my lady and my lady told us to go," said Jockin.

"My mother is hasty and overanxious," said Barbara thoughtfully. "My lord must hear your story with his own ears. Now take me home."

The family looked at one another, but it was obvious there was nothing else to be done. Barbara must be taken back to her parents there and then.

"I will take her, Father," said young Jo. He was about to throw off his colored cap and put on his everyday hood of coarse brown stuff, but the girl insisted he should wear his gay cap with its little bell.

"It will cheer me in the woods," she said.

Plow Jockin's wife was anxious that her husband should go with his son and the girl, if only to do her honor, but Plow Jockin's pride had been hurt; he felt he no longer owed the manor anything. Had they not spurned his noblest offering—his only son?

As for Barbara, she did not want the surly old man to go with her. The light was too dim for her to see if the young man was as handsome as his mother had described him, but he was tall and dressed in gay colors, though the suit seemed somehow odd on him, being so short in the arms and the legs. She felt sure he could amuse her very well on the homeward journey for, after all, a jester is intended to amuse people, that being his lifework, and her uncle's jester could tell most wonderful stories.

She could hardly leave the cottage fast enough.

Being a lady of importance, she did not consider it necessary to thank the poor woman who had sheltered her and bound up her feet. She borrowed the pattens without a thought. She was not a rude or bad-hearted girl, but in her time the poor had to serve the rich whether they wanted to or not, and all such service was taken for granted.

Barbara had a vague idea her father's steward would call at the cottage and reward the woman with a coin or an old robe or blanket. Meanwhile, she thought no more about thanks, and neither did they.

She put her arm in young Jockin's, noticing in the dark how he towered above her, and hearing at each step the jingle of his little bell.

Not being used to pattens, she found them extraordinarily uncomfortable, and being unable to adjust them in the dark, she kicked them off and walked barefoot.

Young Jockin stopped.

"What is the matter?" said Barbara.

"My mother's pattens! You have kicked them away in the dark," said the young man, groping with his own foot to find them.

"What does it matter?" said Barbara impatiently. "When daylight comes you will be able to find them again."

"In the morning I must go to my work. I shall have no time to stop and look for pattens," said young Jockin.

"Then let them lie!" said Barbara.

"They are my mother's only pair," said the young man gravely.

Barbara said no more, his tone was so final. She even pretended to help search, and the pattens were soon found lying in a clump of heather.

"Let them lie there now you know where they are!" the girl suggested, but Jockin would not.

"Someone might take them," he murmured, tucking them under his arm.

"All that fuss for a silly old pair of pattens!" grumbled Barbara. "And there is nobody around to take them, only that shabby old hermit."

"The holy hermit would have no use for pattens!" Young Jockin laughed.

Barbara heard his laughter in the darkness; it seemed to illuminate the forest and warm her through. She remembered who he was.

"Are you really a jester?" she asked.

"I expected to become one," he said gravely.

"Do you like making people laugh?" asked Barbara.

"I never made anyone laugh in the whole of my life!" young Jockin said gravely.

"*What?* Don't you tease people and say witty things?"

"I don't care to tease and my tongue is very slow," said Jockin.

"Well, your mother told me a different tale!" said Barbara. "But if what you say is true, what in the world made you want to become a jester?"

"I was born smiling," the young man exclaimed, in the same solemn manner. "The wise woman put it into my parents' heads and they have never forgotten it."

"It is extremely odd!" said Barbara, shaking her head in the dark. "Then what do you want to do most of all in the world?"

"I want to please my parents!" said the young man, so fervently that the girl was surprised.

"What, more than *anything?*" she asked.

"God could not send me greater joy," said young Jockin truthfully.

Barbara was about to say that *her* dearest wish was to have a handsome knight wear her favors in a tournament and, having defeated all others, ask her hand in marriage and take her away from the dull old manor house to live in a castle. But young Jockin's sincerity touched her.

She remembered her own failings toward her parents, and promised herself that she would take her punishment meekly and try to please them better in the future.

Her tired feet ached unbearably.

"Can't you even tell stories?" she asked complainingly. "Or shall I tell you one?"

As the young man said nothing, Barbara began to relate her adventures of the day.

Her penitent mood had quickly changed, and the tale she told was full of swagger and mock bravery. She forgot her sore feet as she related it, but at the end her companion said nothing.

"Don't you marvel at my adventures?" she demanded, stung by his silence.

"It was a poor story," said young Jockin gravely.

"Tell me a better!" shouted the girl.

"Unworthy of a fine lady," continued Jockin.

"What do you know of fine ladies?" she demanded.

"A tale that does no honor to her parents," the young man insisted.

"Hold your tongue! I thought you were a jester, not a priest!" shouted Barbara.

They both relapsed into silence.

Barbara began to trip again and to cry quietly.

Since the beginning of their quarrel she had loosed the young man's arm, and now she lagged behind him, the odd ends of her hair falling in her eyes, which were already blinded with tears of anger and self-pity. She barged into a tree and fell.

The young man lifted her gently. "I think I had better carry you," he said in the same grave manner.

Barbara was surprised to find him so tall and strong. She did not know how his muscles ached, how his whole body stooped with weariness from the day's long walk, from the bustling, jostling life at the manor, the weary waiting, and the last humiliation.

Barbara's thoughtlessness shocked and troubled him. He only wanted to set her down at her father's house and make his own way back without thought of reward. He looked forward the next day to resuming his laborer's work beside his father, and hoped his mother would put aside forever the dream that had been such a delusion to them all. If the noble people at the manor resembled the haughty (if distracted) mother and this spoiled, wayward child, he dreaded more contact with them and longed for the familiar peace of field and forest.

As for Barbara, she cuddled into his arms as easily as a young kitten, glad to be spared the trouble of walking, and resenting the clumsy pattens he still carried and which nudged her now and then.

The young man would not talk to her, but the tinkling of his little bell made a kind of conversation that fitted comfortably into her half-doze.

It seemed a very short while before she was set down on the village green. A few faint lights in the manor house showed that everyone was not yet in bed.

"You will be safe here," Jockin said, straightening his aching back. "I am glad to have served your ladyship."

He turned to go, but Barbara protested. "Don't go! Come in! Come in! You shall have meat and drink in the hall, and the steward will reward you. Come in with me!"

In a strange way she felt as if Jockin's presence would protect her against the reckoning to come. She was shivering, half with fear and half with cold.

Out of the forest the moonlight shone on the young man's quaint dress.

"Oh, you do look strange!" she giggled. "There—you *have* made somebody laugh now! You must come in and see my father and remind him of his promise!"

"No, my lady!" Jockin was protesting, but Barbara's voice rose louder, and lights appeared in the manor gateway. Two guards ran out, followed by some servants. They saw the Lady Barbara apparently struggling with a tall fellow in odd clothes, and immediately closed with him roughly.

"Don't hurt him! Don't hurt him!" Barbara cried, half laughing and half crying. "Bring him into the manor. He must see my father."

So Jockin passed through the great gateway for the second time that day, but where in the morning he had been a free man, that night he was a prisoner.

One or two servants had run ahead to bring the news. The great hall was thronged with people and torches. They swarmed in from the kitchens and from the rooms above.

The Lady Isabel had been pacing the hall, too distracted to spin, to embroider, or to go to bed. Her husband, lately returned to hear the terrible news, sat at the dais where meals were served, but could eat nothing. Both advanced as the little party entered the hall, and in another moment Barbara was in her mother's arms.

How could I have been so wicked or thought so unjustly of her? Barbara thought, as the usually severe and dignified lady wept over her daughter's shorn head and covered her dirty face with kisses.

Nobody spoke of punishment, save for the most innocent of all, young Jockin, whom the lord of the manor ordered to be flogged and then questioned before his punishment should be decided.

"But, Father—this fellow did not run off with me!" Barbara protested. "He brought me home from the forest where I was sheltering in a cottage—yes, and carried me half the way when my feet were sore."

"Surely it is the same young man who was here this

morning!" said the Lady Isabel. "Yes, I remember his
ridiculous clothes and cap. He had some odd tale about
wishing to serve us in the manor. The poor fellow is quite
crazy, but he certainly could not have stolen our daughter,
since he has been sitting in our kitchen most of the day,
being stuffed, no doubt, by the cook."

"You made him a promise, my lord!" said Barbara, now
in full possession of her dignity as she found herself safe
and cherished in her own noble home.

Turning imperiously to young Jockin, she said loudly
and in a patronizing tone, "Tell my lord your story, good
fellow. Do not be afraid!"

Young Jockin bowed low, but replied, "Indeed, my
lord. My lady is mistaken. I have no story to tell. I would
like to be on my way."

"No, no!" cried Barbara, excited. "Sixteen years ago
my lord made you a promise. Can't you remember?"

"Hardly, my lady, since I must have been a newborn
child in those times," replied Jockin.

"Oh, oh! How tiresome you are!" Barbara cried, dancing up and down. "My lord told you to come and be his
jester—isn't that the truth?"

Young Jockin merely bent his head. For the moment
his parents were forgotten. His one wish was to escape to
the quiet woods.

"Is this so?" asked the lord of the manor curiously.

"My lord has no need of a jester," the young man said.
"I serve with my father on the land. I serve my lord best
wih plow and harrow, my lady has said so."

"The young man is right," the Lady Isabel said approvingly, still fondling her daughter. "Give him money,
my lord, and let him go!"

But the lord of the manor was curious. "Tell me again
when you say this promise was made?" he asked Jockin.

"Sixteen years ago my lord met my father, poor Jockin

of the plow, while out hunting in the forest," Jockin said simply. "I had lately been born. My lord flung a silver coin to my father, and a nobleman beside him flung another. 'Twas then the promise was made. There was a jester also, and he—*he* too was there!"

Jockin pointed at the dwarf, who leaped angrily behind his lady's skirts and began to mutter, "Grinning like an ape! I remember him! Grinning like an ape!"

Sir Richard of the manor suddenly slapped his thigh as the dwarf's angry, excited chatter brought the whole picture before him.

"I call it to mind!" he exclaimed, "The fellow is right! I called his father moonface, and ordered him to preserve his own carcass till he had brought me his son. But has the sickness spared him then?"

"Aye, with my mother and myself, God be thanked!" the young man replied.

"Then your father minds my words better than the rest of my serfs," said Sir Richard, "for half the village was swept into the grave, and only three survived out of the abbey of Nottingham. As for my pages, they are either orphans or things of poor spirit. The sickness has robbed them of parents, wit, and courage. But you, young man, you have the marks of the sickness on you if I see them right. Did you suffer?"

"They say I laughed, and it left me," Jockin replied.

"Stout words for a jester!" approved his lord. "Well, then, are you come to entertain us? Can you leap and dance and tell a merry tale? What have you for amusement?"

The young man was too bashful to reply, knowing that he had little to amuse such a company.

"Let him go!" the Lady Isabel said impatiently. "I love not jesters with their bawdy tales and noisy pranks."

"He is neither witty enough for a jester, nor witless enough for a buffoon!" screamed the dwarf. "In short, he has nothing to show but his motley, which fits him as ill as his pretensions! Send him away, my lord. What need have you of entertainment while your faithful Dobbin lives to tell you tales? Send him away, my lord!"

"Your tales are either stale as last year's bread or full of spite and malice," replied Sir Richard, but his brow puckered in perplexity, for he was a man of honor, and the story Jockin had brought revived his promise of sixteen years ago. He was disappointed in the gawky young man, whose tight clothes were only pathetic, not even absurd. He was so nearly a buffoon, yet the grave dignity of his face forbade men to laugh at him. Where then was his wit? Apparently he had none.

Perhaps he can make himself useful around the house, thought Sir Richard, seeking to compromise, while the Lady Isabel, remembering that the tall, awkward fellow had saved her beloved, badly behaved child, thought, "Out of that ridiculous outgrown costume, he would not be bad-looking. We might use him in the garden."

But Barbara decided Jockin's fate by collapsing suddenly in her mother's arms. Since early morning she had eaten nothing but a few handfuls of wild strawberries and had walked many a weary mile. The long, exciting day had been too much for her, and the hot, crowded hall with the excitement of her return and her parents' argument set her head in a turmoil. Suddenly the manor hall seemed to spin in a circle of dancing stars, and she fell fainting to the floor.

Her mother supported her. Servants carried her to bed. Gruel was brought, her old nurse attended her, and the doctor was sent for. But when she opened her eyes, Barbara only asked for Jockin. She was in a fever and imagined herself in the woods again. The poor young man, left alone and trembling in the manor hall, was now sent for to go to the ladies' apartments and soothe her.

"Where are the pattens?" she kept asking.

Jockin was able to show her that he had them safely. He even closed her hot hand on them to prove they were not lost.

When, late at night, she fell into a troubled sleep, they threw a few rushes for him outside the door so that he could sleep within call if he was needed. He slept more fitfully than poor Barbara, wondering what his future was to be, and worried because his mother would not have her pattens in the morning.

Once he found the dwarf standing over him in the moonlight.

"Go home, poor blockhead!" the dwarf said. "Your place is in the fields. There is nothing for you here. I will show you the way out."

Resentment rose in Jockin's breast at the dwarf's enmity. "I will go when I am bid," he replied in a low voice.

"Once I gave your father a button for you," the dwarf continued. "I said I hoped it might choke you. Did your father tell you that, Sir Booby?"

"My mother sewed it on my cap, to fasten it," Jockin replied. "When it threatened to choke me I threw it away. Do you hear that, Sir Mannikin?"

The dwarf made a kind of hiss, and slunk away to lie before his lady's door. Long afterward Jockin could hear him snoring in the dark.

Chapter 4

Jockin and the Pages

Jockin himself lay awake all night.

He had been more tempted to follow the dwarf's advice than the spiteful Dobbin dreamed. The strangeness of the house, the crowds of servants, the agitation of the evening's adventure, all became part of a world too large and too magnificent for him. He even thought of tiptoeing over to wake the dwarf, and asking whether, after all, the hideous little man would show him the way out of the manor. Then he clutched the wooden pattens and remembered his mother's hopes for him. Already he was well established, lying across his lady's door. Perhaps of their own accord his lord and lady would tell him to be gone in the morning, and then he would have no cause to reproach himself in returning to his parents.

But the night was long and his sleep very fitful. He was glad when daylight came and the nurse appeared at the door with a ewer, bidding him go down into the courtyard and fill it with cold water from the well.

Below, the manor house was astir. Sleepy serving girls swept up the rushes around the central fireplace in the hall, and the cool, sweet scent of morning blew into the frowsty house from a door left open to the yard.

Jockin crouched low, slipping along the side of the long wall, hoping not to be seen, but his colored garments were soon noticed.

"How does my Lady Barbara?" one of the servants asked him.

"I know not!" he stammered, terrified as a little crowd gathered around him.

"Come! Did you not lie by her door all night?" one of the maids teased him.

"I did!" said Jockin.

"Did she not groan and sigh?"

"She did!"

"And cry out, and groan again?"

"She did that!"

"And then, perchance, she fell silent toward morning?"

"Yes, that is so!" said Jockin.

"Or else, on the contrary, she groaned more mightily than ever?"

"Why, that may be so, likewise!" said poor Jockin, utterly bewildered, and only trying to humor them and get away.

"Why! Here is a fellow who knows no difference between sighing and silence!" jeered the servants. "Perchance she snored all night, like Dobbin the dwarf?"

"Oh, no!" said Jockin, shocked. "I'll be bound she did not snore!"

"Well, does she recover?" the servants pressed him.

"Indeed, 'tis likely!"

"Or does she die?"

"Indeed, 'tis likely, too!" said poor Jockin, thinking of the girl's white face and rambling voice as she had lain exhausted on her pillow the night before.

"The fellow is a fool," the servants said. "We'll have no sense of him. Go, ask the nurse!"

Thankfully Jockin went on his way, but the yard was full of pages, as bright-eyed as the maids had been bleary, dowsing each other with cold water as they washed themselves around the well.

"The jester. Ho! The jester!" shouted some of the boys, and Jockin saw here a crowd more dangerous than the maids.

"Where is your bauble, Jester?" one of the boys cried,

twitching the cap from Jockin's head. He still wore the foolish headgear as if he could not bear to be parted from anything that linked him with his home, and now he stood turning his roughly cropped peasant's head to left and right as the cap was whisked and tossed from boy to boy across the yard, the little bell ringing a mild protest at each flight through the air.

"Here is his bauble!" called another, snatching the pattens from Jockin's hand. The boys clustered around, laughing at them and clapping one another over the head with them.

"Those are no bauble! Those are his dancing shoes!" cried one of the pages. "Put them on and dance, Jester!"

"Yes, put them on and dance!" the rest commanded.

Their fierce, strident young voices challenged poor Jockin like an army. Bewildered and terrified, he dared not disobey. But he could not dance.

When the pattens were strapped on his feet he could only stand shamefacedly with his arms hanging down, the empty ewer at his side.

"If he cannot dance, he shall jump for us!" said one of the boys, dragging into the center of the yard a rough wooden bench some four feet long and standing about twenty inches from the ground. "Come, leap over this, Sir Jester, for jesters should leap, and leap mightily. Set down your ewer, sir, and leap for us."

Again Jockin saw nothing for it but to obey. His legs were long and he was light of foot, though the wooden pattens hampered him. He leaped over the bench to the approval of the pages.

"And now leap over the ewer!" said they, setting the ewer on top of the bench and forming a circle so that he could not run away.

"Beware lest you break it and the steward flog you!" they jeered.

Young Jockin had found some of his lost confidence when he cleared the bench so lightly.

By stretching his legs he cleared the ewer, and the pages applauded loudly.

"Good fool! Good jester!" they praised him. "What shall we set him to jump next?"

"The well!" cried a fair-haired squire. "Let him leap the well. If he succeeds, we will let him go."

The well was surrounded by a stone parapet some three feet high by two feet broad. The mouth was a full six feet across. It was a leap any youth might have ventured in his hose, but in pattens the takeoff was heavy, and below, the water gleamed darkly. The bucket chain, falling into deeper and deeper shadow, disappeared at last as if it went on forever.

Hoisted aloft by the pages, Jockin looked anxiously across the well's mouth. The distance seemed infinite and his legs were heavy as lead.

"Loose him from his pattens!" one of the boys advised.

"Aye, loose them. He has leaped his breath away!" several others cried, but one of the biggest, a young squire with a cruel twist to his mouth, objected.

"Why, a little child could leap it barefoot! A boy could leap it backward. Go on, Sir Booby, lift your legs high and wave your arms. 'Twill fly you over!"

He gave Jockin a little push, at the same time tweaking at his jacket, so that his fall was averted. But the momentary loss of balance and the sight of the dark water rising to meet him so disturbed the poor fellow's nerves that his legs began to tremble beneath him, and he fully believed the wooden pattens were chattering on the stones.

"Leap, Jester, leap!" the big squire cried, and before the rest could interfere, Jockin in desperation leaped.

He leaped so wildly that he missed the parapet and fell

sprawling beyond it with grazed knees and hands. The loudly applauding boys ran to pick him up and dust him off with rough kindness, for they were not evilhearted, only a jester was fair sport, and had equal right to make a jest of them when it pleased him.

"Here's a penny for you, fool!" said the biggest squire, to prove his nobility. "I swear I have never seen such a leaping fool in all my life. I vow he never saw the parapet, he jumped so wide."

"What is it? What is afoot?" cried a childish voice, as Philip, Barbara's younger brother, came on the laughing squires and pages. "Has this fool been entertaining you?" he asked, half curious, half jealous of missing any spectacle.

Little Philip with his gray eyes and beautiful face was the darling of the manor house. Soon he was going to his uncle's castle in Wales to be educated as his squire. Meanwhile, he was taught by Father Francis, and followed the older squires with hero worship and envy.

"What has the fool been doing?" he repeated, forgetting that he had been sent to ask why Jockin dallied so long with the water.

"He has been leaping the well mouth in pattens!" the squires related.

"Oh, I should like to see that!" Philip said. "Let him do it again!"

The squires looked at Jockin, sitting on the ground, still panting a little.

"Will you leap again?" one asked him. "He does it right easily," he added to Philip.

Jockin heard the new respect in their voices, and his fear of them faded a little. But his fear of the well increased. Never, never again would he leap that terrible mouth in pattens.

Dumbly he shook his head.

"Tell him to leap!" the boy pleaded.

"Look you, Sir Philip, he has leaped enough," one of the squires told the little boy.

But Philip would not be dissuaded. "I will have him leap!" he insisted.

"Then let it be in his hose—take off his pattens!" a page suggested.

"Come, Jester, wilt leap barefoot?"

Jockin rose gladly, kicking off the ill-fitting pattens. He knew his long legs would carry him twice the length of the leap when they were not fettered.

Little Philip might have been satisfied, but again the biggest squire intervened. "Since he is such a merry leaper, let him leap blindfold, with the full ewer in his hand!" he suggested, and the rest roared their agreement.

"Truly you shall be our champion leaping jester!" they told Jockin, hoisting him again to the parapet with many a friendly slap of encouragement. "Fill up the ewer! How shall we blindfold him?" they cried.

They hauled up the bucket and filled the ewer to the brim. It was not so heavy and Jockin handled it almost with disdain. His success among the boys was exciting him. Blindfolded or not, he could fly the well mouth, and if he cut his knees again, why, no matter. He measured the distance carefully with his eye, determined this time to shorten his leap and land on the broad parapet. Half a dozen pages and squires ran to the far side.

"We will catch you! Do not fear to fall again!" they cried.

Jockin tried not to listen as the empty bucket was returned to the well, falling with a hideous splash into the water far below. The chain ceased to run out with a jerk.

"How shall we blindfold him?" the boys cried.

One boy offered his shirt, but another picked up the cap of motley, lying trampled in the dust.

"Blindfold him with his cap! Blindfold the flying jester!" he said.

Young Philip echoed them. "The flying fool! The flying fool! Jump, Jester, jump!"

They turned his cap back to front and pulled it down over his face. Now he was completely blind, standing somewhere above the dark water.

"Hoodman Blind! Hoodman Blind! Who touches you?" the boys shouted, pretending to tweak his clothes, but the eldest pushed them away.

"Three times I turn you and at 'one!' you leap!" he commanded, suddenly jumping up on the parapet beside young Jockin and swiftly turning him around three times. "One!"

Jockin was facing the opposite parapet exactly as he had begun, but the spinning set his head in a whirl and deceived his direction. Giddy and uncertain, he gave an awkward jump sideways, where he thought the parapet must be, struck the side of the well, clawed at the stones, missed, and fell backward, down, down, down, into the darkness below.

There was a shriek from Philip and a horrified gasp from the pages, who had grabbed at him in vain before he disappeared. They had only succeeded in saving the ewer, which one snatched from Jockin's hand as he fell.

In a moment all their heads were bent over the well's edge, but had Jockin looked up as he fell he could have seen nothing. With the jester's hood pulled down over his eyes, he was Hoodman Blind indeed.

He hit the water with a splash, sooner than he had expected. It closed over his head like a second hood, and the force of his fall pushed him several feet below the water. But a kick from his long legs brought him swiftly to the surface again, and his arms, striking out in terror, caught the rim of the bucket. He found the chain, hauled one leg after the other into the bucket, and stood gasping in his wooden boat, too shaken and terrified at first to push back his hood and relieve himself of this dreadful dark. When he did at last push back the hood, the chain tautened between his hands and the handle began to creak. The boys above had seen his rescue and were hauling him up in triumph.

"Ho, ho! The jester swims as well as flies!" They laughed, ready to be mightily amused by the adventure, now that their fears were over. "Shall we dip you again, Sir Jester, or drop in your pattens so you can walk out?"

But their teasing was friendly, as were their faces when the chain at last hauled the bucket to the top.

"Is our jester drowned?" came the anxious voice of the little Philip, who could not see over the edge.

"Aye, drowned like a kitcat, and here he comes!" said the squires, as the unfortunate Jockin scrambled out of the bucket onto firm ground.

The boys wiped him down and squeezed out his clothes as best they could. Several of them emptied their pockets and pressed into his hand a coin or some small treasure.

Others filled his ewer, and set him on his way with much encouragement and praise.

"In truth, he's a good leaper," they said as he left them.

But poor Jockin's troubles were not over then, for on reaching the apartments where the family slept, he found the dwarf still lying outside his lady's door, apparently asleep, but as Jockin passed, he shot out a foot and tripped him so that he fell sprawling, the ewer breaking into a thousand pieces on the flags.

Lady Isabel could be heard screaming, and the nurse

ran out scolding, while the dwarf chuckled with glee.

Jockin was in a sorry plight when the voice of Lady Barbara weakly summoned him to her room. Grumbling, the nurse went herself to fetch more water in a new pitcher, while the unlucky jester, wet and shivering in his sodden motley, leaving damp footmarks wherever he trod, stepped quietly into Barbara's room to wait on her.

Chapter 5

The Pages' Jest

Barbara had taken a fever, possibly through sleeping in the damp woods all through a long afternoon. She kept to her bed, now feverish, now in a kind of stupor, demanding only her mother and her jester.

She could not bear to see Jockin dressed in anything but his motley, which he had dried by sitting in the sun on the manor parapet. Every now and then she demanded that he should ring his little bell, for the sound was a comfort to her. She would not accept food or drink from anyone else, but lay holding fast her mother's hand and complaining imperiously if Jockin was long out of her sight.

The Lady Isabel, whose gratitude was waning, and who had a natural dislike of jesters, was forced to sit all day, and even part of the night, with this poor fool in his ridiculous ill-fitting garments constantly before her eyes. Her exasperation grew so intense that she sent him there and then to the manor tailor to be measured for a suit of proper motley, with cap and bells that would fit him, and since a bauble was part of the whole distasteful outfit, a bauble he must have as well.

She could not deny that his manners were not so uncouth as one might expect of a peasant laborer, and his gentleness to her child warmed her heart and softened her voice toward him. He might have become a groom to the family's apartments, the lady thought, if Barbara in her illness had not been so stubborn about his costume. Now that the new suit was made, it was a pity to waste it.

Jockin would have liked nothing better than to wait on the ladies in the comparative privacy of the upper rooms. The great hall still terrified him, and he dreaded the main meal at the long table, where all members of the household met and dined together.

The pages were friendly, but teased and baited him with rough good humor. So did the serving maids. Before their quips he felt stupid and helpless, like a real fool, yet he knew he was no half-wit. The pages put their heads together, scheming, and he dreaded a new proof of their high spirits.

Sir Richard ignored him, but he ignored the dwarf too, and all his servants of a lower order. They said he was a hard lord in the village. Nevertheless, his children loved him, and Jockin longed to please him or make him smile. As the days went by and he grew used to the life in the manor house, he lost most of his fears, but he still felt strange and foolish.

The other servants liked him, all except the dwarf, who was more jealous than ever when Jockin's gay new costume arrived.

The rest enjoyed having a butt for their own wit and, finding he bore no malice, thought the better of him and were often kindly as well as rude.

The children of the house, half spoiled and half neglected, began slowly to look upon him as their friend.

But Jockin pined for his home in the forest. After a week in the manor he felt he had been there a lifetime.

One sunny afternoon when the Lady Barbara was recovering, a couch was placed for her in the tiny walled garden where Lady Isabel grew certain herbs for medicines and a few flowers.

Barbara's two little sisters were with her, while Philip played with a pet monkey and frightened tiny Isabel, pretending to make it bite her.

"Now I will teach you to be a jester!" Barbara said, taking the bauble out of Jockin's awkward hands and pointing it at him. "You should not carry your bauble *so,* but *so!* as if it were part of you, not a thing you drag about behind you. And you must not sit as others sit, above all not as a peasant sits, all knees and elbows, but lightly thus—as Philip is sitting, cross-legged and much at ease. Then you must walk upon your toes, and not trip upon the points of your shoes. You should move your head quickly, *thus*—then the bells will ring—and wear a melancholy air only to make other men laugh. You should make a mock of eating and drinking, taking from other men's plates and sipping much liquor from an empty cup. You must learn to play the wit before my lord, not by word of mouth if it does not fit you, but by tumbling and leaping and the making of odd grimaces. Men must always be aware of you. Treat the ladies with great chivalry, but see that every gesture is exaggerated, for that is what they expect of their jester. Above all, listen to all gossip and all adventures and relate it to my lord. He well likes a good story, and that lazy Dobbin is always behindhand with the news."

As Barbara finished speaking a page appeared in the garden, bowed low, and said, "My lady, there are people below wishing to speak with this fellow."

"With Jockin?" Barbara asked in surprise.

"With my lord's jester, said they!" the page replied with a hidden smile.

"Why, who can they be?" Barbara wondered curiously. "How are they, these people?" she asked.

"Monstrous plain people, my lady," the page replied, giggling a little. "I think they may be his parents."

At these words Jockin's heart seemed to turn a somersault with joy within his breast. He started to his feet.

"Not so fast! Not so fast!" Barbara said. "Does my mother know, Alaric?"

"My lady is in the village, visiting the sick," the boy said. "The people I spoke of are in the kitchen. Shall I bid them wait, my lady?"

"I would much like to see them!" Barbara said with curiosity. "I will come down. No, my legs fail me still. Bid them come up to me here!"

"*Here,* my lady?" The page faltered a little. "I do promise they are very simple folk, and this is my lady Isabel's own garden. If her ladies were to see them come—"

"Bring them by the outer wall and up the steps of the terrace," Barbara commanded. "And you children"—turning to her brother and sisters—"you can go."

"I want to see them too!" pouted Katherine, while Philip protested, "If you send us away, I shall tell our lady mother you entertain peasants in her private garden."

"What if you do? She intends to send me to a convent shortly." Barbara sighed. "However, you can stay if you will. Tell them to come to me!" she commanded Alaric.

It was all Jockin could do not to follow the young page, so eager was he to see his father and mother waiting for him below. Instead, he began nervously to dig a hole in one of Lady Isabel's flower beds with the bauble Barbara had returned to him. With all his heart he resented the page's patronizing manner, but he was thankful he had not to receive his parents in the swarming kitchen below, with the maids and squires mocking at him. Here in this little terraced garden it was very peaceful. The children, curious to see their jester's family, were in a quiet mood. Only Philip's monkey chattered, echoed occasionally by little Isabel.

For a long while nobody came to them. Barbara grew impatient.

"Where are they? Has Alaric forgotten? Has my mother returned? Have they not found the way?"

At last she pleaded, "Go down, good Jockin, but when you have found them, bring them directly to me here, by the outer stairs and the terrace."

Jockin was hastening to obey when they heard footsteps and Alaric's grinning face appeared at the top of the stone steps that led down to the outer terrace—the garden being built high within the walls for light and air.

"The parents of my lord the jester!" he announced with an impudent flourish, and disappeared.

Two crooked figures limped into view, one leaning on the other's arm. The old man wore a beard that almost swept the floor, while the old woman, stumbling in filthy rags, nodded and beckoned with her grizzled head and free hand as she clung to her husband with the other. They were an unpleasant spectacle, and Barbara recoiled as they advanced upon her. Jockin perceived in a moment that two of the squires had dressed themselves up to make game of him.

"Are these your parents, Jockin?" Barbara whispered, with disgust in her voice.

"None of mine, my lady!" replied Jockin, catching the "old man" a blow with his bauble that knocked his wig awry and disclosed the grinning face of Gareth, one of the most high-spirited of the squires.

The "old woman" advancing on Philip tweaked the little monkey's tail so that it ran screaming behind Barbara's couch, after which she executed a mock dance and curtsy that set the children laughing all the harder as they saw the trick that had been played upon them.

Their laughter was echoed by a crowd of pages whose heads peered over at the entrance to the garden, but the next moment they scattered to make way for the two imposters, who fled for their lives as Jockin set upon them with the only weapon he had, his bauble, which he wished had been a lash with seven thongs, so great was his rage.

But before he could pursue them far, the pages banged the little gate of the garden in his face and fled pell-mell, the last calling back in some repentance, "Have patience, Sir Jester! Your real parents are here and will be with you shortly!"

Jockin learned afterward that while his true parents waited in the kitchen, the mischievous boys had dressed up two of their company as man and woman, and paraded them throughout the household, their lord and lady being absent, the one with his falconer and the other with the sick. It was a long while before poor Jockin was allowed to forget the gibe that "it takes two sets of parents to bring up a jester," and long before he forgot the pain it caused him.

But this afternoon as his sore heart throbbed with bitterness and humiliation, one of the lower servants again pushed open the garden gate, this time for Plow Jockin and his wife, who stood dumbly transfixed with awe at the sight of the beautiful children and trim garden. Their delight on seeing their son, the very picture of a true lord's jester in his handsome costume, and with a new bauble in his hands, was mingled with bewilderment at finding themselves in such strange place and company, instead of gathered in family fashion around the smoky fire of their own cottage in the forest.

With peasant incoherence none of the three spoke or greeted each other. Plow Jockin performed a lurching kind of bow to the Lady Barbara, while his wife bobbed a curtsy. The three younger children stared.

"Are you fed?" Barbara asked them, remembering the responsibilities of a lady of the manor.

"Aye, my lady, the cook has fed us well," Plow Jockin replied.

Silence again fell.

"I remember you," Barbara said to the peasant woman. "You bound up my feet, but I was very ill for all that, after. We have your pattens still. Go fetch them," she ordered Jockin.

The young man disappeared in search of them. He would have liked to explain to his parents how he could not leave the manor to bring them before, also to have told them the adventures they had brought him, and the manner in which he had come to wait upon the Lady Barbara and wear a new suit of rich material, but it was not necessary to explain to his mother. Nothing surprised her; everything had fallen out just as she had expected. Here was her boy set fair for success just as he ought to be. It was only that dunderhead, her husband, who had muddled affairs the first time he took the boy to the manor. And after all, it had all turned out for the best. She stood staring after her son with an air of wondering admiration that anyone could have thus brilliantly fulfilled his destiny. It was her husband who inquired after the Lady Barbara's present health.

"I have been sick almost unto death," she said, "but I am now recovering. My spirits are still low and I need much to divert me."

She was unused to playing the invalid and found it highly entertaining.

"And our son? I hope he amuses your ladyship?"

"Well, as for that, he is not very amusing." Barbara sighed. "He does not know how to quip or jest and seems too melancholy to leap and gambol. But I am acquainting him with such tricks as befits my lord's fool, and no doubt he will improve when he is longer among us."

Plow Jockin nodded all the while she spoke, but the mother's eyes strayed toward her son, now returning with the pattens. The Lady Barbara's words meant nothing to her. She could see with her own eyes what a splendid person he had become. She resolved to call upon the wise woman and tell her how her prophecy had come true. And if, as she expected, young Jockin were to give to his parents some of the handsome wages he was surely earning, she meant to spare the wise woman a penny for being so wise.

But so far Jockin had earned no wages. The head steward had questioned Lady Isabel about it and she had ordered him to wait until Christmas. "The lad may not stay with us, and meanwhile his motley has cost a pretty penny."

Young Jockin had nothing to put into his mother's hands but the poor pattens he had cherished for her and hidden under a floorboard from the prying eyes of his fellow servants.

The little monkey had been scampering up and down behind Barbara's couch, chattering angrily at the sight of more strangers. He had not forgotten the tweak given to his tail by the first comers, so that the sight of Plow Jockin and his wife drove him into a frenzy. He chattered and danced, and when for one moment Jockin's wife turned her back upon him, made a single spring that landed him upon her head.

The poor woman shrieked and dropped her pattens.

On the terrace fell a shower of flat bread cakes she had brought for her son, and they rolled in all directions.

Little Isabel shrieked too. Katherine hid her face in her hands. Philip went very white but snatched at the monkey, who bit his finger severely.

Plow Jockin stood with his mouth agape, but young Jockin seized the monkey by the tail and angrily flung it up onto the terrace wall, where it continued to gibber and rage, tearing the Lady Isabel's roses from their boughs and hurling them down among the cakes scattered around Barbara's couch.

Consoling his mother, Jockin did not at first see that his young mistress was lying back on her rich cushions, laughing till the tears ran down her cheeks.

"Oh!" she gasped at last. "Oh, how I was mistook—but quite mistook! Never in one afternoon have I been so greatly entertained. In sooth, my poor fool, if you cannot make me laugh, at least your parents can!"

Young Jockin flashed her such a look of fury that she quailed.

"How now? Why do you fix me so?" she asked indignantly. "Did I set the monkey on her? It is my brother's monkey, not mine. But to see it perched there on the old woman's head! I could have split my sides. You should laugh, too, Jocko, not fix me as if I were at fault."

"Your ladyship *is* at fault to laugh thus at my mother!" Jockin heavily replied.

His mother put a frightened hand on his sleeve of motley. This was not the way to speak to noble ladies. She half expected Barbara would dismiss him instantly. But instead her eyes became round with amazement.

"It was such a comical sight!" she protested. "And why should I not laugh?"

"If the monkey had attacked your lady mother—would you call it comical?" Jockin sternly asked her.

"*Comical!*" At such a terrible picture all laughter left Barbara's face. She could hardly bear to imagine such an adventure. Why, the whole household would suffer for it and the monkey would most certainly be killed.

"Oh, no!" she stammered. "But then, my mother is lady of the manor, not just a poor peasant woman!"

Plow Jockin and his wife nodded vigorously at Barbara's speech. She was perfectly right, of course, and Jockin's boldness shocked them. They began to edge their way out of the garden.

Young Jockin, scarlet with humiliation and anger, made as if to follow them.

"Where are you going?" Barbara cried sharply. "Do not leave me!" But when she saw Jockin's face she flinched.

"I am going to see my parents on their way," he said, so finally that she could only grumble, "Then do not go beyond the first mile in the forest!"

Baby Isabel was left playing with the flat bread cakes on the terrace.

The father, mother, and son did not speak as they left the manor house, traversed the village, and entered the woods.

Plow Jockin was content enough. This was the way the world was made. A rich man, a poor man; the world for the rich man, what he did not want of it left for the peasant. His son had done better than most for himself, and one should help one's children, even at the cost of the ditch filling up again with weeds and the hoeing being a lot more than he could tackle, with the rheumatics that came upon him nowadays. His wife was always urging him to ask more wages for the work he did, now that men were scarce and the land crying out for labor, but Plow Jockin was not a man to take advantage of his lord's difficulties. He plodded on in his slavery as before.

Plow Jockin's wife was content because of her son's splendor. The young Lady Barbara had hearkened to him, the spoiled minx, when his mother had expected him to be beaten for his boldness. She did not resent the monkey's attack, nor Barbara's laughter, though she had been frightened enough at the time. But it was an excellent thing to amuse the young lady and make her laugh; a scratch or two was well suffered if it helped her son's position. She was glad to have her pattens back, and one day Jockin would bring her some money.

But young Jockin strode angrily between his father and mother, his back turned forever on the manor house, so he decided. The trick the pages played on him, the monkey's attack on his mother, Barbara's laughter and haughty words, all had humiliated him almost beyond endurance.

The cool woods soothed him. Comfort came with the scent of the pine trees, the soft soil underfoot after the stone flags of the manor, the silence of loved company after the noisy, thronging halls.

He would rather be a poor peasant on his own land, he thought, than a rich slave in his lord's manor. His bells, vibrating ever so slightly at each step, reminded him of his bondage. He would not go back.

But the serene calm on his parents' faces smote his heart. They expected so much of him! And they were so content with him as he was now.

Every step took him farther from the manor, closer to his home. He determined to mend the roof for his father, to make his mother a little garden where she could grow herbs like the Lady Isabel. Oh, the warmth and comfort of that little house and imaginary garden after the great manor. But never again—never, never again.

Now his parents stopped in the middle of the path.

" 'Tis time you should turn," Plow Jockin told his son simply. "The Lady Barbara was unwilling you should leave her, and the first mile is long past."

Looking from one parent to the other, Jockin read in their faces the joy with which they sent him back to his good fortune, saw, too, that on neither face, not for the fraction of an instant, was there any doubt that he did not wish to go.

"But, Father—"

"The sun is setting," Plow Jockin said. "You should return in haste to your lord and lady. We will come again to see you."

Helplessly young Jockin watched them go home without him. He had not the courage to disappoint them.

Yet the thought of returning to the manor nearly broke his heart. He wondered if he should run off to join the band of outlaws that he knew roamed the far forest, and never see anyone again. But no, that would break his mother's heart.

Wearily dragging his feet, he proceeded toward the manor house in the gathering dusk.

As he entered the gate he saw the dwarf, and turned aside into the little chapel in order to avoid him. The priest, Father Francis, who was chaplain to the manor, was polishing his holy vessels with a cloth.

At first young Jockin did not see him. Tired, dispirited, and homesick, he leaned against the wall and let the tears run down his face. When he looked up the chaplain stood beside him.

"What is your trouble, my son?" he asked with sympathy but with some sternness. "Are you crying for some unconfessed sin?"

"In truth it is a sin to seem to be what one can never be!" cried the poor boy. "I am neither wit nor half-wit. How can I ever be a jester?"

The priest gave him all his attention; for some while he had watched the youth in his unsuitable dress, a jestless jester—had noticed his sweet temper, popularity, and good influence over the squires, the maids, and even the children of the manor. He had seen how the dwarf's influence, somber and unkind, was waning, and had pitied the innocent peasant boy, so misplaced and so mishandled by his fellow servants.

"What can I do?" the poor boy now sobbed. "If I leave my lord's employment 'twill break my mother's heart, yet stay here I cannot."

"Why not?" asked the priest.

"I do no good in my profession; I have no heart in it," said Jockin.

"Then set your heart there," said the priest sternly. "God will help you," he added.

"Why, God has no blessing for jesters!" said Jockin.

"You are wrong, my son. God blesses all men in their proper work. Does He not warm the earth for the plowman, like your father, and provide acorns for the pigs that your mother keeps? Why should He not bless the jester who keeps his lord in merry mood?"

"I cannot be merry!" sighed Jockin.

"My son, by your own confession you have not put your heart in it. Ask of God to help you. Keep your heart open to God, your ears and eyes open to what goes on about you. Find out what men laugh at, so you may supply it to them. Ask advice of older men, for jesters should be wise as well as witty. See how other fools act—help yourself to your best advantage. God has already given you a good head, and in the manor all men already trust you. Men prefer a good friend to a good fool, and many a man's fool has become his friend."

Young Jockin was comforted by the priest's advice. He left the chapel after a fervent prayer to God to help him in his strange profession, and strode down the hall with his head so high that the dwarf, who had intended to shadow and mock his awkward country gait, was forced to run, and became himself the butt of the impudent pages.

The Lady Barbara was back in her own apartments, with tears still glistening on her fever-wasted cheeks. She held out her hands to Jockin, all her pride and dignity forgotten.

"Oh, Jockin, dear Jockin! I thought you had left me forever! I felt sure you would never come back, your face was so angry when you went away. I am sorry I laughed at your mother if it hurt you! Philip should have his monkey whipped! And those hateful pages! I cannot think what my father will say to them! Why, your parents were not nearly so dirty and unpleasant as they were!"

"Do not tell my lord, dear lady!" Jockin begged her. "They meant no harm; it was but a trick for laughter-making, and as you say, they in no wise resembled my parents."

"They *did* look odd!" Barbara said, beginning to laugh again at the memory, while Jockin in his lighter mood now saw the joke in a new light and began to smile with her.

Sir Richard, visiting his daughter, found her thus laughing with her jester and gave the boy the first nod of encouragement he had shown him since Plow Jockin brought him to the manor.

Later, at supper, young Jockin again came to his notice when the dwarf in spite tipped him off his bench. It being the part of jesters to tumble and fool around, the whole hall found this amusing, and when he rose to the surface with his face plastered with a special kind of cream cheese for which the cook was famous, even Sir Richard slapped his thighs and called him to his side to pour his ale.

From that moment onward, young Jockin found a certain confidence that helped him to perform such tricks as pleased the household.

As he grew more friendly with the other servants, he was not afraid to question them. Many had visited in other houses and could tell tales of minstrels, jesters, and tumblers they had seen and heard, how one acted like this and another in that manner; how one was dismissed for rudeness to his mistress and her ladies—"For a fool may be monstrous impudent, but he must never be sincere in his discourtesy"—and how another became the friend and adviser to a king.

He discovered a form of puppetry that mightily amused the children. Enfolding his fist in his hood, and with a few pieces of stick and stone to help him, he made nodding heads that mimicked and grimaced and waved mock arms. He showed them the chaplain preaching, so kindly and true that no one could laugh in malice, the steward giving orders, and the cook's men staggering with great dishes for Sir Richard's table. He made for them little Isabel nodding asleep on his knee, and Philip's monkey with its comical ways.

The younger pages clustered around to watch, and they were soon joined by the older squires. The servants of the hall peeped over the squires' shoulders; the ladies peered to see what was amusing them so long and could see nothing but the grimacing face of young Jockin mimicking his players.

The Lady Isabel, angry at finding everyone so distracted, sent them about their ways and scolded the jester.

Jockin sat in misery for an hour bewailing his fortune. First he could not jest and now he might not. But a page came to him from the nurse.

"The young Lady Isabel has a pain in her cheek; her nurse is asking for you."

Then he picked up his sticks and stones again, tucked his fist inside his hood, and ran to amuse the little teething Isabel. This was a labor that he gladly performed, and when he saw her asleep on her nurse's knee with the pain forgotten, he counted himself the happiest of men.

Chapter 6

Arrivals at the Castle

The Lady Barbara was now fully recovered, and peace
had settled on the manor house.

For a while Barbara did her best to please her mother
and behave as one might expect Sir Richard's eldest
daughter to deport herself. She sewed for long hours, sang,
and fidgeted at her mother's side while the Lady Isabel
discussed interminable lists of household necessities with
the housekeeper.

Because she knew her mother disliked him, Barbara
even neglected Jockin, but her eyes wandered enviously
after her little sisters as they followed him around or perched upon his knee.

Jockin grew very fond of all the children. It was easier
to laugh when they were there. When they were awake
they never let him alone, and Jockin felt the better for it.
His eyes grew brighter, his step firmer. He was no
longer afraid to tap the pages on the head with his bauble.
He learned to answer them back lightheartedly, tit for tat.

He taught himself a trick that made him very popular.
He put six pages in a line shoulder to shoulder with their
heads bent to touch their knees. He leaped the length
of this line with his great leap and his legs spread wide
apart, giving the final page such a backward push that the
whole six sprawled head over heels. The onlookers demanded this again and again, and six pages were always
ready to be overthrown, for Jockin's push was not a rough
one and boys have no objection to tumbling about.

72

As the weeks went by, Jockin was surprised to find how dim and distant seemed his life in the forest. Then a day had seemed an eternity, spent working at his father's side while the sun crept its slow course across the heavens, and often no word was spoken between them from sunrise to midday.

Now it seemed he was hardly out of bed before it was evening, and each day fled faster than the last, full of action, of talk, of comings and goings, of difficulties greater and smaller, of successes and failures, of hopes and disappointments.

One morning a new spirit of excitement stirred the manor house. The children ran about shouting for joy; the squires began to pay more attention to their doublets, and to practice more assiduously their exercises with sword and charger.

The Lady Barbara, though more dignified than her younger brother and sisters, followed her mother with a radiant air, while the Lady Isabel was positively smiling.

Presently, while her mother was busy with one of her usual long confabulations in the kitchen, Barbara slipped back into the hall and sought out Jockin, who was binding up the paw of an injured wolfhound. The dog was licking his hand, but when Barbara stooped over the injured paw, it began to growl.

"Savage brute! It will bite you, Jockin," said Barbara.

"Not savage, but sad and sore," said Jockin, continuing to tie his rags. "It will be many days before Ludovic can hunt again."

"Then my father will be angry," said Barbara, "for my uncle is coming this week, and Ludo is my father's best wolfhound. He will be sorry not to show him off to my Uncle Simon."

"Perhaps he will recover quickly, after all," said Jockin, fondling the dog, who yearned to lick at him with its great wet fangs.

"All the animals love you, Jockin," said Barbara wonderingly. "Perhaps they feel that you, too, are a bit silly, as they are. And you are not so very silly, are you? I wonder what my brother will think of you. For my brother Edward is coming with my uncle, from Wales. He has been his squire these many years, and soon will be a knight. He is my mother's favorite son. Have you not noticed how pleased she seems since we had the letter from my uncle?"

"Indeed I have noticed it," Jockin agreed. He was always glad for someone else's pleasure.

"And beside my uncle and my brother, my little cousin Francis is coming as page to my father," Barbara went on. "He is the youngest, and they say my aunt breaks her heart at parting with him. I saw him, three years back; he was a weakling then, and my brother says he will never break any lance but his own. Father Francis will instruct him and he will be brought up with the other pages. In exchange my uncle will perhaps have Philip at his house, as he has had Edward. At least, that will be discussed while they are here."

"And that is not the only matter they will discuss," said Philip, joining the group. "I have heard that my Lord Simon, my father's brother, will visit my aunt at Shrewsbury, where she is lady abbess, on his journey to us, and will discuss when she may be ready to receive *you*, sister. Perhaps we shall travel back in company together— who knows?"

Like most children, they both disliked the idea of leaving home and living in new surroundings. They taunted each other to console themselves, and both grew angry.

"My uncle will never receive a rude, ill-mannered boy like you among his squires!" flashed Barbara.

"And what will the sisters say to your cropped head?" mocked Philip. "They will think you mean to take the veil indeed, and they will never let you out!"

"And I have been so good!—so good ever since!" wept Barbara, rumpling her short locks.

"My brother Edward was a year older than I when he first left home," Philip said, half in gloom, half in pride, but Jockin heard the desolation in both young voices and remembered his own heartache and longing for home, which still tormented him from time to time.

"It is good to go into the world," he said gently. "I, too, wished that my parents would not send me away, but here I am, and now I have new clothes and new learning, and a good house to live in, and fine company."

"But I already have plenty of new clothes and a good house to live in—not like yours!" said Barbara, wrinkling her nose at the memory of the hut in the woods. "And as for company, what shall I do in the midst of all those solemn nuns?"

"You won't be there so very long," said Philip, more kindly. "When they have taught you all a lady should know, Mother and Father will find you a husband and you will be married."

"And have a manor house of my own," said Barbara, brightening, "and you will come with me to be my own jester, will you not, Jockin? Promise me you will! You will have learned so much by the time I come out of the convent!" She sighed.

"I don't see why you should have him!" grumbled Philip. "A man has first right to his father's possessions. You always think Jockin belongs to you. Why shouldn't I have him when I marry?"

"Well, Edward comes before you!" said Barbara. "But in any case Jockin really belongs to Father because of the promise, you know. And Father doesn't want him, neither does Mother; I don't believe they like him at all. I shall simply ask father if he will give him to me on my marriage, because I am older than you are, but when your children are teething or your dogs' paws need tending, I will lend him to you, for nobody is more loving with children or more tender with animals than Jockin, although he is not such a very good jester!"

"Oh, well, in any case I shall be off to the Crusades by then," said Philip, moving off.

The manor house became such a hive of activity that before, in contrast, it had almost seemed to sleep.

Messengers were sent to the farms that belonged to the manor house, and to peasants and serfs that owed any duty to their lord. All kinds of game and meat came in, poultry, cream, and cheeses.

The best carpets, brought from the Orient by Crusaders, or bought from rich traveling merchants, were laid on the floors, and rushes strewn where there were no carpets. Piles of logs were brought in to dry in the hall, so that the central fire should not smoke unduly when they were used.

The best linen was aired and spread in the guest chambers. The squires, already pressed for space, were crowded to make place in their quarters for such other squires and pages as could not be housed with their lords.

The Lady Isabel, still with an eager smile on her thin lips, unfolded a tunic from her richest chest and laid it out for her eldest son, with a belt, splendidly jeweled, and a matching brooch to wear in his cap.

Sewing women made new dresses for the little girls, while Barbara was allowed a full long skirt in a rich material like her mother's, and a golden net to hide the tragedy of her hair. This last gave her great consolation and pleasure, for while her head was so ugly she could not forget the sorrows and shame of that day in the forest.

"Does my Lord Simon bring his jester with him?" Jockin asked young Philip at last. It was a question that he had been longing to ask ever since the first announcement of Lord Simon's coming, and he did not know if he hoped the answer would be aye or nay. He had a great desire to meet a real established jester and study his manners, but he feared to be ridiculed by all the company in comparison, and on the whole he hoped Lord Simon would leave his jester at home.

"I do not know," said Philip. "Old Eustace is very old, and last time he came he picked a terrible quarrel with our dwarf. But my uncle is exceedingly attached to him and I daresay he will be here."

However, when the brightly mounted company rode into the manor courtyard one cold and sunny afternoon, every color was represented except the motley. Old Eustace, it appeared, cripped with rheumatism, was remaining at home to comfort and entertain her ladyship, who was taking hardly the loss of her youngest son, now riding out in his father's company to begin his education first as page and then as squire to Sir Richard, his father's brother.

Barbara and Philip, waiting with their mother at the manor's entrance, quickly picked out their cousin, for among the sturdy squires bearing Lord Simon's coat of arms he alone wore a new doublet on whose breast and sleeves were embroidered the arms of their own manor house.

"He is half a head less than you, Philip, though he is a whole year older," Barbara whispered, and they gazed rather scornfully at the young page boy dismounting from his tall horse at the gate, but the next moment their attention was taken by their brother, who had become such a grand and splendid fellow since last they saw him that they could hardly believe it was the same Edward who used to race them up the pear tree by the wall, and who once owned the pony that now belonged to Philip.

Sir Richard had ridden out to meet his brother. His servants mingled with the strange company, and at the manor entrance, villagers and peasants goggled at all the bustle and the splendor.

Jockin stood beside the children and his lady, goggling like the villagers, while young Philip, entranced, forgot his manners.

"Go and hold my lord's stirrup!" Barbara told him impatiently.

The words were meant for Philip, but Jockin heard them and thought the order was for him.

Ashamed, he ran forward with Philip at his elbow, both jostling to reach Lord Simon's horse before he dismounted.

Jockin's long legs carried him faster, but he cleared a way through the crowd for Philip, who flew like an arrow behind him. When Philip saw he would not arrive before the jester, he gave Jockin such a push from behind in his exasperation that Jockin missed the stirrup and plunged headlong beneath the horse's belly, arriving at the far side with his legs in the air.

Fortunately for him, Lord Simon's horse was docile. He seemed to agree with the opinion of the crowd that a jester in cap and bells is born for such foolishness. He merely pricked his great ears and stood like a rock while Philip triumphantly held the stirrup for his uncle to dismount, and the unlucky Jockin staggered to his feet.

He expected blows and curses, but found the crowd laughing, while the clap Lord Simon gave him on the shoulder was not unfriendly.

"Where did you find this merry knave, Brother?" he asked Sir Richard. "My poor Eustace would have broken his neck had he played such a trick on me."

Sir Richard smiled half contemptuously, for he had not seen Jockin's tumble—and then suddenly a full, warm smile transformed his face, the smile his children loved and which made Jockin his slave.

"Why, he was born my jester, and you should know the tale!" he told his brother, taking him by the arm. "Come into the house, and I will tell you about it!"

From that day Jockin felt Sir Richard had acknowledged him, and that he belonged to the manor house.

Chapter 7

A Jester's Revenge

Jockin could imagine no greater pageantry or splendor than that which now filled the manor house. Feasting continued late into the night. Such tricks and leaps as Jockin had practiced he had to repeat till his legs were almost too weary to lift him off the ground, but if he fell his lords applauded even louder, giving him tidbits from the table and sips from their wine cups till his head spun madly.

After all, it was an easy thing to please noble people, Jockin thought, walking on his hands the length of the banqueting table.

He trusted his hands and feet farther than his poor, slow tongue, when it came to entertainment.

When the dwarf, jealous, began to make spiteful remarks, the guests urged him to imitate Jockin, and after breaking a couple of wineglasses he retired into the shadows and sulked. Jockin rolled him a few spiced cakes off the table, but the dwarf threw them back again, growling with anger.

All was feasting and celebration, yet Jockin was surprised to hear the squires and pages grumbling.

"All talk, talk, talk, this year! It was not so at other times! My lords do little but discuss the difficult times, the cost of their establishments, the education of their children, and the unreasonableness of the peasants! My Lord Simon complains that his land is becoming a wilderness for lack of labor, or that he must pay vast sums to bribe the peasants to work on it. And Sir Richard boasts he will have neither bribery nor wilderness, but will force the laborers back to the land. They discuss risings and the temper of the people. What subjects for a banquet!"

Jockin remembered the days of hoeing and the long, long hours fighting the weeds that blew from the ditch, weeds that seemed to grow taller between sunrise and midday. He remembered his neighbors' strips of land, many abandoned since the Black Death, many reclaimed by their lord, so that the laborers left had to struggle harder and harder against the weeds.

Some of the peasants who had bought their land and were freemen had demanded high wages for this increase in their toil, but Plow Jockin had always lacked initiative, as his wife moaned when she heard of other people's gains. The Statute of Laborers lately passed by Parliament, which forced the same low wages on all and sundry for harder toil, did not comfort her. She felt that even the Statute of Laborers had something to do with Plow Jockin's being so easy to please, and her prayer of thankfulness was for her son Jockin who was slave to no one, but a jester in his lord's house.

Once a month Jockin was privileged to go home through the forest to spend an evening with his parents. His mother always managed to find a special dainty for their humble meal, if it was only a couple of eggs, and in his turn Jockin brought a bundle of scraps handed to him in the kitchen, which were often hoarded by his mother and eked out till his next visit. In spite of the long hours and the toil, Jockin's parents thought that they fed like kings now their son was at the manor house. Jockin knew better, and found the food coarse and plain after Sir Richard's table, but he enjoyed his mother's flat bread and the small rare eggs better than anything he ate when he was away from his home.

He would have had much to tell them had he been a talkative boy or if his father and mother had asked him questions, but it was not their way to chat much together. They sat around the smoking fire when supper was over, quietly content to be together, till it was time for Jockin to return, and then, having kissed his mother, he would leave the hut and walk back with his father to the elm halfway to the village, where they parted and went their own ways.

"Where do you live, Jester?" Lord Simon's squires asked him.

They were a lively set of boys, and the story that had been told them of the trick played on the jester by the squires of the manor household tickled them mightily.

"In the forest," Jockin replied.

"Far from here?"

"A third of a day's journey."

"When do you go next to visit?"

"Three days from now."

"Will you take us with you? We would fain see a jester's home!" cried the boys, half in earnest, half in jest. "Are there masks hung in the doorway and bells on the roof? Is your mother a merry wife, is your father a clown?"

"Nay!" said Jockin, smiling at the thought of these high-spirited boys in their brilliant doublets inside his mud hut. "With three of you inside it, my hut would tumble down!"

"It would split its sides with laughing, no doubt!" cried one of the pages. "But take us, Jockin, so we can boast at home we have been to a jester's castle!"

Jockin shook his head and smiled, wishing he had not mentioned his coming holiday, for the boys continued to pester him and plead whenever their duties to their master left them free, and when the younger children of the manor heard them they joined in the chorus and besought Jockin to let them come and see his home.

"For my sister Barbara has seen it, and walked the whole way there and back again," said Philip. "And nothing will she say about it—just to torment me!"

Fortunately Jockin's holiday dawned on a feast day, and no one expected a mere fool to attend the service. As many of the manor-house people and their guests as could be crushed into the little chapel were busy there with Father Francis, leaving a mere handful of squires and pages dawdling about the courtyard in the cold winter sunshine.

These Jockin avoided by entering the kitchen, where a scullion handed him the usual bundle of scraps saved for his parents. Then, his heart lighter for having escaped the squires, Jockin left the manor by a back entrance and began his long walk home.

Whatever had been the trouble and turmoil of the month before, a great feeling of peace always filled Jockin's heart the moment he entered the woods. He forgot the noisy manor house, the teasing pages, the spiteful dwarf, and the busy, bewildering life behind him. The peace would stay with him all the way to his home and again all the way back to the village and the manor house until he left it behind in the courtyard.

But today the peace did not last long.

The cool, dim light of the trees had scarcely wrapped him about before he heard laughter and excited boyish voices behind him. Half a dozen squires and two or three pages (younger boys of less than fourteen years, in attendance on the household) were scampering after him through the trees. When he turned toward them they pre-

tended to hide behind boles of trees, peeping out like so
many mischievous squirrels, and slipping from trunk to
trunk when they thought he was not looking.

Jockin's first thought was to run after the leaders and
drub them soundly, but the woods were wide and the boys
lively. He caught one and cuffed his ears, but the rest
laughed and mocked and dodged him like so many monkeys. Meanwhile, the sun moved across the sky and his
holiday was hardly begun.

I will give them a walk for their pains that will rack
their young legs! thought Jockin, setting out for home at
a great speed, but the squires were well trained in all kinds
of exercise and physical fatigue. They held on at a distance like so many young dogs of the chase, calling mocking words if he turned around, and daring him to come
and prevent their visit to his jester's castle.

It merely wasted his time to dodge them among the
trees. One or two of the pages fell back, but the older
squires took the smaller ones on their backs, and it was
wonderful what pace they made. Jockin could see they
were all of the visiting household, save one small page
who bore his own master's arms, and who he was Jockin
could not tell.

When he came to the elm, which was his father's point
for turning back at night, the boys were still at his heels,
and poor Jockin feared they meant to keep their word
and come all the way with him. What his parents would
say to the laughing, lordly throng of squires he could not
tell, but a fierce kind of pride filled him with resentment.
He would not show them his home. It was the one secret
place left him in his life. Secret and peaceful it should
remain.

He knew his father would not come to meet him, for
he would be working on the land till darkness fell. When

time allowed, Jockin would go to help him before the evening meal, but twilight fell early in the winter, and either might arrive home first, or both together.

Sometimes his mother came a little way to meet him but never farther than the first bend in the path past their home.

Suddenly he remembered an empty hut, almost as big as their own, which stood forsaken in the middle of the wood at no great distance. In his despair he wondered if he might not lure the squires inside it and shut them in till he came back again. He remembered the late owner had cut down some trees around the hut, and there might still be some boles lying about.

It was a chance without much hope of success, but Jockin did not hesitate to take it.

Suddenly turning aside, he began to run through the trees like a deer.

The boys were plodding along well in the rear now. The path was well trodden, and they had little doubt it led straight to Jockin's home. If he arrived well before them, they would get there a little later, that was all.

But his red-and-yellow motley was too conspicuous to miss; in fact, Jockin did not wish them to miss it.

With a shout the boys left the path in pursuit and followed him through the trees, shouting in mock indignation at his daring to try to escape them.

Jockin found it simple to outdistance them; he knew the woods well and could leap and run like a wild thing in the forest. He knew he was soon out of their sight, because here the trees grew much closer together, but if he dodged them now and made for his home, they would guess his trick and presently return to the path and follow him.

His home was now so close that they might quickly

come upon it if they followed the track, but the hut among the trees was also near at hand, and by showing himself now and then and running on, he was able to keep the squires heading in the right direction.

Then, when the clearing was only a few hundred yards ahead, he put on his greatest speed and arrived at the hut so far beyond them that their questioning shouts came faintly through the trees, and he guessed they were searching, and would take a little while to overtake him.

The hut was better than he had expected, for the mud floor had cracked, sunk, and become a pool of black water. And the door swinging on rude hinges was solid, to keep the warmth in a peasant's home through the long stern winter.

The wooden latch was high. It still held, and would not be easy to find from within once the door was closed and the hut in darkness, for there were no windows and the cracks were stuffed with mud to keep out the cold.

And as Jockin suspected, a few boles of trees still lay close to the mud walls where the peasant tenant, smitten with the Black Death, had left his work forever. Jockin seized one log and then another, dragging them close to the door with all his strength, but leaving the door wide open to swing clear of them.

The voices became louder as the squires' search pressed forward. Jockin slipped behind the hut, his heart beating. If he could not stop them now, he determined to return to the manor house and lose his holiday. His mother would look for him and be disappointed, but better wait another month than suffer humiliation and embarrassment from this crowd of feckless young rascals. Jockin had the memory fresh in his mind of how the manor pages had made game of his parents, and had no doubt these older squires could amuse themselves just as heartily at their expense.

A shout rose nearby as somebody spied the clearing. "A hut, a hut! It is the jester's castle!"

Other voices repeated the cry as Jockin heard them run into the open space around the hut.

"Ho, Jester! Ho, Jockin! Are you within?"

"Indeed it is his home! I last saw him vanish in just this direction, and see! See! Here is his bauble!" cried one of the boys, picking up Jockin's toy, which he had laid on the ground when he shifted the tree trunks.

"Ho, Jockin! Ho, Jester! Come out and welcome us! We have found you—you cannot escape us now!"

"He is afraid of us!" said one of the squires. "But what a home to hide in! I'd liefer keep a pig in it! Ho, jester! We are coming in your house to find you!"

"Send the pages in first, and when he has laid about them, he can take us on!" cried one of the biggest, laughing—but Jockin could tell by their voices they were afraid to meet his swinging arms again, and the boy who had spoken first was the one whose ears Jockin had cuffed. "Nay, we will all go in together. Put the pages in the middle!" cried another.

" 'Tis mighty dark!" one remarked, evidently sticking his head through the door. "And it has a most unpleasant smell. . . ." But the rest of his words were drowned as the boys surged into the dark hut, only to land with a floundering splash in the dirty pool that had once been the mud floor.

They were struggling on hands and knees in six inches of water when Jockin slammed the door to behind them, and dragged the heavy trunks against it. He added a few more for good weight, wedged them with chips, and, disdainful of the boys' shouts and curses, ran through the glades to the proper path, not stopping till he reached his own hut, one mile and a half farther on the way, and found his mother wondering at his lateness, since his father was already home, this winter evening.

For once she questioned him, wondering at his flushed cheeks and panting breath, but he put her off with descriptions of the bustle at the manor that had kept him, the new arrivals, and the banquets that had continued all the week.

Too quickly the quiet evening passed beside the fire, and he must exchange the friendly squalor of his home for the splendor that was so vast and cold.

He could not ask his father to let him go home alone, and he could not return without visiting the hut where he had locked the pages, though he had little doubt that they would find their way out, even if they had to lift off the roof to do so.

So when they parted at the elm, young Jockin gave old Jockin time to pass out of sight and hearing and then took a shortcut through the trees in the bright winter moonlight.

Sure enough, when he reached the hut the door was flung wide open and the trunks were scattered. The united weight of strong young limbs, afraid of darkness and captivity, had burst the barricade, and the boys were gone.

All except one.

Jockin found a shivering page, half asleep and half perished with cold, wedged in the warmest corner he could find, between the door and a tree trunk. He still clutched Jockin's bauble in his hand as if for company.

Jockin's pity welled up for the child—he was no more than that—as he saw his swollen eyes and heard the exhausted sobs that shook his narrow chest. To his surprise, he saw that he bore Sir Richard's arms. He must be the new page that had lately joined the household.

"Why did you not escape with the rest?" Jockin said, chafing the poor boy's hands.

"They ran so fast—they would not carry me any more!" said the boy. "They knew you had tricked them. They ran after you and tried to find the path again. But a holy hermit came and rebuked them; I do not know what he said, for I was behind the rest, but they fell away then and said they would be going home. I tried to follow them, but the way was difficult and they went so quickly I got left behind. I wandered for hours until I found the hut again. I would not have found it, only it was full of moonlight. I would have died, Jester, had you not come to find me. Indeed, I think I am likely to die now!"

"Nay, nay! Look up and stamp your feet and clap your hands—thus!" said Jockin, pulling the boy to his feet. "Now take my hand and run beside me till the blood tingles inside you once again. Once we are at the manor, the lady housekeeper will give you a hot posset, and you shall take no harm. How came you to run so far with such tall rough lads as these, and all to torment a poor jester?"

"I did not mean to torment you," said the boy, sobbing. " 'Twas the rest set about it, in the courtyard, while the others were in chapel saying their prayers. I said it was a shame and unkindness to follow and bait you, and I was for telling my cousin Philip in the chapel, that he might tell my father and prevent them. So they took me with them by the arms, and then rode me on their backs that I might not tell, but when we fell in the black water they let me go, and afterward they would not carry me anymore."

"I will carry you, when the blood runs more hotly!" said Jockin kindly. "For I see you had much kindness toward me and I thank you for it. I had wished you might have found my father's home, for there at least is shelter and a dry floor, as others have found before you," he mused, thinking of the Lady Barbara that previous night. "But step you out well, for the night is no longer young, and maybe the seneschal has closed the gate upon us."

"I think there will be trouble when we return," said the boy with some satisfaction, "for my father will be angry with our squires for treating me thus, or, if he is not angry, my mother will upbraid them instead. But I shall not be there to hear it"—he sobbed with a sudden burst of tears—"for I must stay and learn to be squire to my uncle, and I like it not here. I wish to go home!"

Jockin's sympathy went out toward the poor boy, who, like himself, had so many difficult lessons to learn in his new home. Yet how could the lot of a wealthy young nobleman compare with that of a poor jester?

"Have courage!" he told him. "I, too, left my home with much sorrow to learn my way in life. Already I weep no longer, and Father Francis has told me how best I shall succeed. You should consult him, young sir page, for a wiser man does not breathe in all the manor."

"Oh, I daresay I shall meet him often enough," said the boy, "for he is to instruct me, along with my cousins. But tell me, Jester, how did you come to leave your home? For no jester that I ever saw jests so little as you. Our Mad Eustace, even in his rheumatics, makes fun and torments us. Yet you are not sad. I would say there is about you something of that comfort men feel when they have jested well. Yet it is no jest. You do not often smile."

"If I learn to smile, will you do the like?" Jockin asked kindly, smiling in the moonlight, for he felt this page would tread a lonely path among his peers. "Will you teach me to laugh so we may share it together?"

"I do not think there will be much to laugh at over

there at the manor," said the page. "My uncle is fierce. My aunt scarcely looks at me. My cousins despise me. I do not care to laugh at common jests as jesters do commonly perform, and such as do make ordinary men laugh."

"Then we will have our secret jests and tell them to one another," said Jockin, rather to encourage the boy than from serious intention. "For a jester who can please no ordinary man and a man whom no ordinary jester can please should certainly be friends. And I will tumble and joke as before, but you may know that this is my secret jest, since I jest at jesting!"

The boy laughed out loud at this, and Jockin thought, How is it that in such simple company my tongue runs so smoothly? I had not dared to speak such nonsense before my lord.

He could feel the hand within his begin to glow with warmth, but the page's legs trailed sadly, and presently Jockin took him on his shoulders, till his feet in their wet shoes froze again, and so, between walking and riding, the pair returned to the manor. There the hall was filled with slumbering bodies clustered as close to the fire as space allowed, for drafts cooled the hall and rushes are a mean protection on a winter's night.

Young Francis slipped away to the pages' quarters and Jockin to his sleeping place, an alcove above the stairs, close to the family's apartments. He no longer slept outside the Lady Barbara's door, since Sir Richard was his lord and master, but the dwarf jealously guarded his lord and lady's chamber and opened one inquisitive eye as Jockin found his bed and prepared for the night.

Chapter 8

Encounter in the Forest

Sir Richard took his brother and elder son to ride around his estates. With them rode young Philip, the Lady Barbara, and many of the household. As was the custom of the day, Jockin the jester went with them, mounted on a small white donkey. The dwarf, on a black pony, trailed behind them, craving for the fire in the manor hall and ignored by his masters.

Young Jockin knew little of riding, but his donkey was quiet. He jogged along comfortably enough beside the gay company.

The two brothers spoke seriously about the conditions of the land and the troubled times through which they were passing, but young Edward joked with Philip and Barbara and even with Jockin, till at least half the party was as merry as the rest were sober.

The long ride took them to the very outskirts of Sir Richard's land. They passed the fields where Jockin had worked with his father, and leaped gaily across the ditch that had doubled their labor with its crop of weeds. In the distance Plow Jockin was driving the team of eight oxen on the communal plot. He stared at the company from the manor, and no doubt his failing eyesight picked out the motley and rejoiced at his son's good fortune in being one of this fine procession. Other peasants stared, too, but in sullen curiosity. Few doffed their caps, even when their lord rode up to speak with them. There were not many on the land, and these turned away as if the noble company meant nothing to them—only when it had gone by they looked after it and muttered.

"You see the temper of the people," Lord Simon said. "It is the same on my estate at home. They crave for more money and yet more, but will not work. Since the statute was passed I can find no freeman to work willingly for me unless I bribe him in defiance of the law. And if I bribe one, I must bribe another—therefore, of what use is the statute to us? But your men do not look as if you bribed them, Brother Richard. A more unwilling crowd I never saw, or more threatening. You should watch your interests."

"My interests will survive without bribery," said Sir Richard carelessly. "If they will not work for the statute wage, I take back their houses and refuse them timber. I shut the manor door to them, and give them no medicine for their children. My land, as you see, is well plowed."

"I doubt not you will have a blighted harvest, if not this year, then next," said Lord Simon, "for our father's peasants loved their master, but these men do not love thee, Brother, and in Wales I can only buy their love with bribes. The Black Death killed more than men, Richard; it killed our feudal heritage."

Jockin, who was riding close to his master's heels, listened to this conversation, but the next moment he noticed a movement in the bushes at the edge of the field and turned in his saddle to see what was hiding there, for he was used to watching everything that went on in fields and forest, and nothing escaped his attention.

Crouching in the brambles was the swarthy figure of John-of-the-Field, a hairy-faced neighbor who often plowed beside his father. His face bore the now-familiar sullen expression as he peered at the riders, but when he caught Jockin's eye he scowled angrily, flinging a clod of earth at him with all the strength of his brawny arm.

Crouched as was John-of-the-Field, the clod went astray. It hit the horse that Barbara was riding full on the flank, so that it reared and plunged before bolting between the horses ahead and up the forest path as fast as it could gallop.

The whole party set off in pursuit, except Jockin, whose donkey was in no way suited to join in such a mad chase.

After a few steps he reined in suddenly, turned about, and set off in pursuit of John-of-the-Field, who was running back toward the ditch as fast as he could go.

"John! Ho! John-of-the-Field!" Jockin shouted, kicking his donkey to such a speed that at last he overtook the man. "Do you see what you have done in your madness? My Lord Richard will have you flogged for this, you crazy pate!"

Fear passed like a white reflection across the man's face. Then came anger.

" 'Twas not meant for my young lady's nag, though I'd gladly see Sir Richard and all his children walking barefoot in our forest. But 'twas meant for yourself, you craven milksop! You, who are content to leave your father and your friends to work and die of working, that you may fatten yourself at the manor house, making the gentry smile!"

"My father sent me to the manor, and I left no friends like *you* to die of working!" replied Jockin. "Sir Richard is a just man. He gives alms to the poor and obeys the law. Parliament has set the laws, not my Lord Richard."

"He'll not survive them long," muttered the peasant, scuttling into the cover of the ditch as the sound of returning hoofbeats caused Jockin to wheel his donkey quickly around to see who was coming back.

It was only the dwarf, who shouted loudly, "Did you catch the fellow, Jester? Did you catch up with him?"

"Nay, I caught him not," Jockin said, loyal to his one-time neighbor, "and the clod was not meant for the Lady Barbara. It passed so close to my nose I vow it was meant for me."

"If we catch him we can tell my lord a different tale and he will reward us," said the dwarf, eagerly trotting his pony up and down among the bushes, but Jockin remained still, and John-of-the-Field lay like a hare in his form, so that the eager dwarf did not catch a glimpse of him.

The whole party now jogged back down the forest path, the Lady Barbara in their midst, her color brighter for the adventure, her palfrey docile at last, the sweat drying on its glossy neck. Her elder brother, who rode at her side together with her father and uncle, cast sharp glances on either hand to discover the assailant that had threatened her.

Their attendants quartered the bushes and even searched the ditch, but in the hubbub and confusion John-of-the-Field slipped away and Jockin could presently see his burly figure on the far horizon, busy with his hoe.

"Did you see who flung the stone at the Lady Barbara, Jester?" Sir Richard asked. "Did you see a man escaping over yonder field? You were here meanwhile; have you naught to tell of him who threatened my daughter?"

Tongue-tied as ever before Sir Richard, his loyalty bitterly divided between the old life and the new, Jockin could only stammer, "I saw no one throw any stone at my Lady Barbara; I saw no one escape across yonder field; I have naught to tell of anything that I have seen."

For in truth he had only seen John-of-the-Field threaten himself with a clod of earth, and when the peasant escaped by way of the ditch his back had been turned, and what he *had* seen he did not intend to tell.

"I would swear he was talking to somebody when I

came up with him!" piped the dwarf shrilly. "For I did hear his voice plainly speaking as if he were addressing one with whom he was acquainted."

"With whom were you talking, Jester?" Sir Richard asked severely, with so fierce a scowl that poor Jockin quailed within. "And why did you not follow us when we pursued the Lady Barbara? Speak, fool! With whom did you hold speech this ten minutes past?"

Again poor Jockin's loyalty pulled him in two directions, and again his answer was half-truth.

"I did but speak with my ass," he murmured. "I was but counseling him to return in pursuit of my lord, he being most unwilling to set either foot foremost."

The roar of laughter that greeted this explanation saved Jockin from further questioning. Only the dwarf did not seem satisfied, and he grunted angrily when Edward suggested that the horse had been frightened by a tumbling fir cone or branch of a tree.

"And no harm is done, so let us proceed homeward," Edward said, "for these dark woods seem to me sadly lonesome if even a jester has to speak to his ass for company. Besides, my appetite grows monstrous, and my sister should rest, following her adventure."

So they rode jingling home to the manor house, while Jockin resolved to keep his ears and eyes open, lest John-of-the-Field had a meaning to his mad words. Moreover, the temper of the laborers had changed more than he had thought possible in the few months he had been at the manor house, and even his father, whom he felt sure was working over there on the horizon of the land, had not risen from his work to give his lord a greeting, or notice his son, but had presently retreated out of sight.

Chapter 9

The Jester's Entertainment

Young Philip was to ride back to Wales as page to his uncle.

The pride of his new status overruled his pain at leaving home. He peacocked in the hall with Lord Simon's coat of arms embroidered on his vest and sleeves, taking care to mingle with his uncle's squires as if already he were one of them. He looked contemptuously at his cousin Francis, who made no attempt to hide his homesickness and his envy of Philip's good fortune in returning to that dear home he missed so badly. Even Lord Simon rebuked his son for lack of manly bearing. "He will be better when we are gone," he told his brother.

Sir Richard clapped the boy kindly on the shoulder to encourage him, but he had no use for puling pages and secretly rejoiced in Philip's boldness, little knowing how he, too, would miss his home when the woods and fields of the manor grounds gave place to wide Welsh marches.

They rode away early on a morning that whispered prematurely of spring, leaving the manor house empty and sad. Barbara was mourning her playfellow, Philip's monkey was moping in a recess, and little Isabel was calling alternately for her brother and her uncle, of whom she had become very fond.

Lady Isabel retired to her room and was not seen for several days. Sir Richard had accompanied his brother and sons as far as Shrewsbury to complete the arrange-

ments with the Lady Abbess that he had already begun.
It was expected that her aunt would receive Barbara in
the convent at Easter.

Barbara almost wished it were sooner, the house seemed
so empty, so cold and bare without her brothers and all
the gay company. As for her cousin Francis, he was never
seen without red eyes and a woebegone expression. She
could hardly bear the sight of him.

Jockin's sympathy went out to both the lonely children.
He lay awake at night thinking out a scheme to amuse
them, and so well did he succeed that within a few days
Barbara's eyes were bright again, and Francis smiled and
took notice of what went on around him. Even the monkey
seemed to have new life and ran to sit on Jockin's
shoulder as once it had sat on Philip's.

On bright mornings this little company met in the
small stone garden under the pear tree, and on cold
evenings they shivered in a recessed hall that led out of
the large central hall of the manor. Only the reflection
of the fire reached them; their light was the light of
torches fixed into the walls. They kept their feet warm,
or less than cold, with straw spread on the stone flags,
and Barbara wore a linsey cloak around her shoulders.
But so absorbed were they in their employment that not
the bitterest winter night could drive them to the fire.
Jockin and young Francis, used in turn to the rigors of
a mud hut and of the bleak Welsh marches, thought little
of the cold, but Barbara was accustomed to all the comfort the manor house could offer in winter weather, and
only her pride and a deep interest in what Jockin was
doing kept her in the cold recess, with a tapestry hung
across the entry to shield them from prying eyes, and the
beautiful leaping, roaring fire screened from view. She

rubbed her chilblained hands and stamped her feet in the straw, wishing that Philip were there to join them.

For Jockin was preparing a circus of the animals, the like of which the children had never seen.

Bearbaiting they had witnessed, and they had seen tame monkeys, also falcons and dogs trained for sport, and horses for the tournament, but now with infinite patience Jockin the jester was teaching the animals of the manor house a series of actions and tricks that they would presently display to the household.

It was a prospect that made the long winter evenings fly on wings and kept the children breathless with excitement.

Jockin's patience and gentleness at first astonished them.

"Beat him!" Barbara advised when the monkey sulked and would not do as he wished. "Wring its neck!" she ordered impatiently when her pet pigeon refused to fly back to her shoulder.

Francis added, "In Wales my father had a great hound that would leap a fence. When it would leap no longer, he had it destroyed!"

It was an age of roughness and cruelty to man and beast, but that was not Jockin's way. Ludovic, the hound whose paw he had tended, had become his devoted slave.

Jockin taught him to feign death completely—lying so still and prostrate on the straw that one almost saw the glaze of death covering his eyes. Nor would he stir for any word but Jockin's. When that word came he sprang to life with such a deep-throated bark that the rafters rang and the man-at-arms at the outer gate looked right and left for strangers coming.

Jockin stretched a pole between two stools and himself

ran along it. Then he called the monkey, and the little
fellow followed just as confidently. Jockin then trod the
pole again, but swayed and made as if to fall from one
end to the other. The little monkey waited his turn and
then imitated him while the children held their sides and
the younger pages on the far side of the tapestry almost
died of curiosity to know what all the laughter was about.

Needless to say, Francis would not tell them, though
they made up for their past neglect with such friendliness
and good cheer that he was hard put to resist them. In
the end, six of the best pages were invited to take part
in the pageant. They were the envy of all their fellows.

Frost and snow put icy bars around the manor house.

Jockin missed a visit to his home, the snow was so
deep in the forest. The land lay desolate and untended.
Hunger and discomfort reigned in cottage and mud hut.
Only the houses in the village were within reach of the
manor kitchen, and scraps were not so plentiful nor so
generously given as in warmer days. The hungry dogs
snapped up at a meal food that would have kept a peasant
family for over a week.

Jockin knew that his mother was thrifty with the food
he brought her, and she had her hens. He did not think
she would go hungry. There was a lot of meal the cook
had given him last month because it had weevils in it.
Common people could not afford to turn up their noses at
weevils. No, his parents would not starve during this cold
spell. Jockin was glad he had brought a large supply of
wood to the house on his last visit—in spite of the frost
and snow, their fire would burn brightly.

So he gave his attention to his animals and waited till
the weather should improve, to visit his family.

They brought Jockin's white donkey indoors and
drilled him. He proved a clever pupil, and Barbara

begged to bring her own palfrey, but Jockin dissuaded her. "A hall is no place for such a noble beast, and we have no room to practice him," he said. "In the summer we will teach him some graceful manners out there on the grass."

"But in the summer I shall no longer be here to ride him," said Barbara, her face clouding over.

"Then I will teach him all manner of new ways for your return," said Jockin, to comfort her.

Now Barbara and Francis were eager to know when they could give their performance to the household. They had none of Jockin's patience and regarded each trick as perfect before it was half learned. They marveled at the times he repeated each new performance, and did not know how often he practiced when they were not present, always gentle and patient, rewarding each success with a morsel of food, his praise sufficient to raise each dumb creature to an ecstasy, his reproof enough to send Ludovic slinking under a bench, brokenhearted at displeasing his beloved master.

At last the evening chosen for the performance was at hand. Barbara flew around the household announcing the great pageant that Jockin was to perform. Francis boasted among the rest of the pages, telling them enough to whet their appetites, but no more.

Barbara persuaded the nurse to allow little Isabel to sit up later than usual. Her mother had a headache and had retired to her apartments, as she did so often since her sons had left her. Barbara had sent her little sister Katherine to beg her mother to attend, but the message came back that the Lady Isabel did not think there would be anything to amuse her in a jester's tricks.

Barbara sighed, and when her father, who was expected home in the evening, failed to return at the expected hour, she stamped her foot and said the show would not take place.

Katherine and Isabel cried, the pages looked mournful, the older squires turned on their heels contemptuously, as if such child's play did not amuse them in any case, while Francis found enough spirit to argue with his cousin Barbara, who was now also his lady, and Jockin waited patiently behind the arras with his animals, ready to appear or to be dismissed, as Lady Barbara commanded.

In the midst of this disturbance, the head forester and one of his men strode into the hall asking for Sir Richard. They dragged between them a man from the forest, muffled in what clothes he could find to protect himself from the wintry weather. His face was peaked from the cold and his nose red, but though people went hungry, they did not starve so often in these days, and the man did not look ill fed.

"We caught him knocking the game off the trees with this stick!" the forester announced, holding up a stick in one hand and a bag of half-frozen birds in the other. "Sir Richard will have plenty to say on this matter, and if this fellow keeps his ears he will be lucky! Where is my Lord Richard?"

"My father is from home. We expect him tonight," Barbara replied, taking her mother's place with dignity. "Ho, steward! Give a meal to these foresters and let them wait my lord's coming." Then, with a sudden change of mind, she turned toward her waiting troupe of performers and cried, "Jockin! We will wait no longer. Let the performance begin!"

The household hastily took up convenient positions on benches and stools or seated themselves along the edge of the great dais at the end of the hall where Sir Richard, his family, and his servants took their meals at a great oak table.

Between the dais and the enormous central fire Barbara beckoned the performers to appear, so that they played like black shadows or silhouettes, projected against the firelight. Barbara stood in the center with her arms outstretched and her palms wide. Then from the recess stepped out six pages, each bearing a silver dish at arm's length. When they marched abreast of Lady Barbara, each opened his dish and out flew a white pigeon. These rose high into the roof of the great hall, then, with a clapping of wings, flew down to perch on their mistress's outstretched arms and hands. It was a pretty scene, gilded by the firelight, and Barbara had thought of it herself.

The household roared its applause, and they were still applauding, with Barbara standing with the pigeons on her arms, when Sir Richard strode into the hall.

"What is afoot? Is this a masque?" he asked, shaking the snow off his garments onto the rushes. He thought his daughter Barbara looked very beautiful standing there in the firelight holding the pigeons, so he prepared to sit down and watch her.

But the head forester claimed his attention with his captive.

"Father! My Lord Richard! Father!" Barbara protested in an agony of impatience. "The animals are waiting, and Jockin can scarce hold the dogs in leash! Let Dickon wait till we are done!"

She expected a harsh rebuke, but Sir Richard listened indulgently, waved the forester aside, and sat himself in his own chair with one arm around his second daughter Katherine.

"Jockin!" Barbara ordered, tossing the birds free. "Bring Ludovic!"

Jockin brought the great hound and laid him flat at a word. When it seemed that the dog's great heart had ceased to beat, the pages brought in the smaller hounds, who lay down likewise at their teacher's command, heads between paws, their eyes fixed watchfully on Jockin.

When they had lain thus for three or four minutes, the jester suddenly gave a word, and every dog sprang up on his haunches, Ludovic alone giving voice to such a bark that little Isabel screamed. Seated now like six statues, the dogs still watched Jockin, who gave a peculiar call. Immediately the pigeons flew down from the rafters of the hall, where they had been resting, and perched on the dogs' heads.

Squires, pages, and servants goggled and murmured in admiration. Not a dog snapped at a pigeon or took his eyes from Jockin's face.

Barbara looked triumphantly at her father, but Sir Richard seemed puzzled, half interested and half annoyed. He watched intently the pages picking up the pigeons and carrying them behind the arras, after which Jockin rewarded the dogs with small pieces of meat and led them away.

The pole was next brought, and the hall rang with laughter at the antics of Philip's monkey mimicking Jockin in his feats of balance. This time Sir Richard, too, roared with delight, enjoying no less the little white donkey, who trotted obediently about the hall, stopped and lay down to the jester's order, hopped over a bench with his little unshod feet, and at last leaped over Jockin's back as he bent down in the middle of the hall.

The dogs were now called back, and while the donkey in his turn stood still, the dogs jumped over his back, and finally the little monkey climbed up by way of the donkey's tail and cantered around the hall clinging tightly as the donkey kicked up his heels and shook his head from side to side.

Barbara and Francis, who were merely showmen to this

circus, nevertheless felt very proud of their display, and when it was over looked for their lord's approval.

He gave it generously, clapping the jester on the back and asking for more.

"My lord, there is no more," Jockin said, crestfallen. "It has taken long weeks to train these beasts, and more they could not learn in so short a time."

"I'll warrant you have ruined my hounds as it is!" said Sir Richard, partly in good humor and partly in vexation. "If Ludo and the rest fail to kill a boar for me in the morning, when we go hunting, I'll have you whipped, you impudent jester. But what is left to entertain us? Where is my dwarf? Now, dwarf, show us what you can do, for surely you have as good a bunch of tricks as that little monkey of Philip's. I have it! Throw a bearskin on him and the jester shall lead him while Ludo baits him. We will have a bearbaiting to end a merry evening!"

The dwarf, who was terrified of Ludovic, turned pale with fear. Barbara began to protest, for she did not like this rough and cruel play after the lessons taught by Jockin. Francis looked even more frightened than the dwarf, for he, too, was afraid of Ludovic when roused.

At that moment Jockin spoke up bravely. "Nay, my lord, Ludovic is too noble a hound to bait a bear. That is for small-fry that snap and snarl in the marketplace. Let me play the hound, and the bear shall hold his master's stick and defend himself as best he may."

A bearskin was found and a staff put into the hands of the unwilling dwarf. Jockin went down on all fours and the crude play began, Jockin playful and teasing, the dwarf spiteful and angry. He would have landed many a painful blow on the jester's head, only the bearskin hampered him, and presently when they were both panting and exhausted, Sir Richard called them to stop.

The forester, who was impatient to return home, had been pressing close to Sir Richard's elbow for some while. He now took the opportunity to claim his attention and told his tale.

Refreshed, warmed, and amused, Sir Richard was in no mood to pass judgment that night, though he knew punishment was deserved.

"What shall we do to you, knave?" he asked the stocky peasant, who, in spite of his impending fate, had laughed as heartily as any at Jockin's animals.

"Can you amuse us also?" Sir Richard asked whimsically. "For if you can prolong this evening's entertainment for us, I vow I will let you go free."

The man saw his opportunity, but his peasant wit was slow, and he could only stare and shake his head, his mouth hanging wide open.

"Say aye to my lord and come behind the arras!" Jockin murmured at his elbow.

"Aye, my lord!" the man muttered obediently, following the jester down the hall while the foresters scowled at seeing their victim escaping, but they dared not protest or show their impatience.

Barbara and Francis ran after Jockin, but in the smaller hall he bade them leave him.

"If you wish to save this poor man's life, or at best his ears, go back and seat yourselves and lead the household in much laughter!" he advised them.

A little put out, they obeyed, but the household needed no encouragement in the scene that followed.

Jockin merely went through all his tricks again, adding the poacher to his actors. Counseled by the jester to strictly imitate the other animals, the peasant became a hound with the dogs that feigned death, a donkey with the prancing ass, a monkey clumsily copying the jester. At a word from Jockin the pigeons perched on the man's bewildered head and shoulders, and his puzzled face drew roars of laughter from everyone in the hall.

When the clumsy performance was at an end, Sir Richard was in far too good a humor to have the man punished.

"The credit was the jester's, but 'twas this foolish knave entertained us!" he said, and the foresters relaxed on being rewarded with money. All three left the manor house together, the peasant still bewildered at the turn for the better that his fortune had taken.

Chapter 10

Jockin at Home

The snow melted as suddenly as it had come. The long weeks of forced inaction were forgotten as spring came caroling through the woods, flooding the glades with warm sunshine, while the birds burst themselves singing songs they had forgotten all the winter long.

The occupants of the manor house rode out again; the peasant returned to his plow. Jockin the jester walked home at last to his father's house in the forest. He carried a large sack of provisions slung over his shoulder under the cloak that hid his bright motley, while with his free arm he picked up the best boughs he could find for burning when he reached home. The winter storms had brought down many branches and even some trees. From time to time they blocked the path and Jockin had to step over them on his way. All this combined to make his last visit to his home seem a long, long time ago.

He found his parents well, and helped his father mend a hole in the roof before the wintry dusk closed about them. Then as usual they sat around the fire, silent and comfortable, the only sound the crackling of the burning branches, which Plow Jockin's wife stirred from time to time with her shoe.

But they were ill at ease, his parents. Jockin noticed it in the way they looked furtively at him, his mother twisting her hands in and out of her homespun skirt.

He wondered what could be troubling them, whether they reproached him for being so long away, or if it was some private trouble with which they did not wish to burden him.

Every time he met his mother's eyes she looked away. If he caught his father's glance, Plow Jockin immediately stared at the floor.

At last he began to question them, hoping they might speak of their trouble.

"Did you fare badly this cold spell?"

"Nay, we fared not badly."

"I could not come to see you on account of the snow."

"Aye, we knew that."

"Has the head forester paid you a visit, or anyone else since I was here last?"

"Nay, we have seen no man."

But he sensed their guardedness as they spoke, and even at that moment someone knocked on the door.

Jockin's mother sprang to open it, holding back her son, who would have been before her. The draft blew clouds of smoke from the fire and, coughing, Jockin could not see who stood outside.

He heard a murmured voice, and then his mother's speaking low. "Nay, he comes not!" Another murmur, and his mother repeated, "Nay, he comes not tonight, I tell you!"

The visitor did not seem satisfied, and presently Plow Jockin's wife turned to beckon her husband. As her eyes rested on young Jockin, he saw for a moment they were full of fear.

There was further muttering on the threshold and then the strange voice inquired, "Is that your son within?"

"Aye, it is our son," Plow Jockin agreed.

"He who is jester to the lord of the manor?"

"It is he."

Then Plow Jockin was pushed aside as a bearded face

peered around the door. The face scrutinized Jockin for a moment, then withdrew.

"So you come not, neighbor?" the voice repeated.

Plow Jockin must have shaken his head, for the door closed and the footsteps died away.

It was so little the custom of the family to ask questions that Jockin said nothing, but wondered deeply on what errand the stranger might be expecting his father to accompany him. Neither of his parents mentioned the matter again, and presently it was time to start back to the manor. Jockin's mother stood on tiptoe to draw the cloak around the shoulders of her tall son.

"Does the life please thee yonder?" she asked suddenly, holding him by both arms and looking most anxiously at him. "Dost thou never crave to return and work beside thy father as before?"

Jockin heard such earnestness in her question that he was deeply puzzled. Almost, it seemed, she was begging him to come back to them. Yet she was so pleased with the position he had made for himself at the manor, and when, in an unusual burst of description, he had told them of the success he had had with his animals, her eyes had shone with pride and joy.

"In sooth, Mother, when first I found me there I liked it very little," said he, "and I would have found great delight in returning to the land. But now it likes me very well and I do find many friends around me. Moreover, the pay is good, while those who toil as my father does are poorly paid and go hungry in winter. Methinks I can help you much better as jester than as laborer, if that is what pleases you too, Mother."

"Aye, it pleases me right well," said his mother with no pleasure in her voice.

Plow Jockin added hoarsely, "Do they say at the manor house that the laborers are badly paid?"

"Nay, my lord says not so, he does but obey the laws of Parliament, which has passed a new statute, saying all men's wages shall be thus and thus, nor any higher. But I did hear the squires that came from Wales discussing the matter, and my Lord Simon, Sir Richard's brother, did vow he had to bribe his men to reap his harvest."

"If Sir Richard thought a little that way, men might not bang on people's doors at midnight!" cried his mother angrily, but Plow Jockin hushed her.

"Tush, woman! Do not speak. People fare ill who slander the lord of the manor. It is our duty to serve him, as it is the duty of Parliament to make our laws."

"At least in Wales they think the same as we do!" cried the woman eagerly. "Perchance it may reach the King's ears, and the statute may be altered!"

Plow Jockin shrugged his shoulders and beckoned to his son. They left the hut together.

One mile and a half from his home, when they were nearing the elm where father and son were used to part company, Jockin saw a red glow in the distance through the trees.

"Do you see that, Father? Who can be burning a fire, and such a fire as is yonder, at this hour of night?"

"I do not know. It is no concern of ours," Plow Jockin replied, looking neither to right nor left.

"It comes from the direction of old Lob's hut," said Jockin, puzzled. "Do you know, Father, if the winter snows and storms left it still standing?"

"As I know it, the old hut still stands," replied Plow Jockin, stubbornly tramping on.

Young Jockin had a great longing to make off through the trees and find out what fire burned so brightly at so late an hour, but he could see his father had no such intention. So he determined, when they parted at the elm, to retrace his steps when his father had gone, and seek out the mysterious blaze for himself.

But other plans were afoot that night.

They parted almost wordless, as usual, but hardly had Plow Jockin's footsteps died away in the night before two men stepped out from behind the elm and seized the jester by the arms.

Chapter 11

Jockin in the Forest

It was not in Jockin's nature to shout for help, and he could not struggle. One large hand was pressed over his mouth, while his arms were held behind him.

For a few moments he stood a dumb prisoner between two motionless assailants; then the hand was suddenly jerked from his face and he was turned around and given a push forward.

"Come with us," said one of the men in a low voice. "If you struggle or shout, this club shall quickly silence you."

He brandished a thick cudgel in the dark as they marched Jockin through the trees in the direction of old Lob's hut. So he was going to see who burned the fire whether he liked it or not! Jockin felt a certain excitement and curiosity.

His captors were peasants, not foresters; that he knew at once by the smell of their clothes and their general ill-kempt appearance and manners, even in the darkness.

They stumbled more frequently than Jockin did in the woods, and he guessed them to be men of the fields. He felt them start and curse in nervous terror when branches swept into their faces or twigs crackled extra loudly beneath their feet. Certainly they were not at home in the forest, and he wondered what could be their business there.

Now the glow of the fire could be seen through the trees, and the blaze from it lighted their way so they no longer stumbled. Soon they were within the circle of felled trees outside the old hut, where a fire of logs burned brightly and a dozen or so men sat on the fallen trunks, their rugged faces glowing in the flames.

They looked up and nodded in satisfaction when the two men brought in Jockin. He recognized several faces that he had last seen tilling the strips of land belonging to Sir Richard. He also recognized John-of-the-Field, who sat chewing a twig, refusing to lift his eyes to Jockin's face.

The leader of this little band beckoned Jockin to sit down on a tree trunk near him, and questioned him hurriedly and curtly.

"Thou art Jockin, son of Plow Jockin, who lives yonder?"

"I am."

"Thou art become jester to our lord of the manor?"

"I am his jester," said Jockin, and felt pride surge through him as he said it.

"Since when art thou become a jester?"

"These five months past."

"Wilt thou now leave thy place and return to work with thy father and his friends on the land?"

Jockin merely shook his head without replying.

"Why not?" the man demanded.

Jockin gave the same answer he had given his mother. "Because I can better serve my parents in the manor house. A jester is better paid than a laborer."

The men growled angrily and he felt their anger. He saw their hands clench sticks, and clubs, too, and wondered what they would do to him.

But John-of-the-Field spoke quickly. "Small blame to any man who works where he is best paid," he said. "So the manor likes thee well?" he asked with a certain cunning, and Jockin nodded briefly.

"And is that which I heard say the truth," John-of-the-Field pursued, "that Lord Simon does pay his men twice that which Sir Richard pays *his* men?"

"I know not if it is twice," young Jockin answered. "I did but hear Lord Simon say he had to bribe his men to work. While our lord of the manor did proclaim his men worked loyally for the lower wage and his land was in fairer tending than his brother's."

The men merely growled at this. "Aye, loyal on empty stomachs!" Jockin heard, and, "Sir Richard does not care if we work our fingers off, so that his land is plowed."

The leader was now addressing him carefully. "How many men-at-arms does Sir Richard keep at his gate these wintry nights?"

"Two at each gate and two wardens within," replied Jockin, remembering how Philip and Barbara had told him that in less peaceful times their grandfather had guarded his castle with a whole company of men-at-arms and a drawbridge over a deep moat. But that was before the modern manor house was built, and these days people rode away to fight crusades in other countries instead of attacking their neighbors.

"And does the crooked pear tree still stand against the wall in the outer garden?" the man went on. "I helped my father build the wall that supports the pear tree, for Sir Richard would not have it felled when the house was built. Does it still bear fruit?"

"It does, to my belief," said Jockin.

"How high would you say the pear tree is now grown?" the man pursued.

"Twelve feet would not be far out," replied Jockin, puzzled and disturbed at the man's persistence.

"And the wall, if I remember rightly, is near that height also?"

"Pear tree and wall stand of equal height," Jockin agreed, uneasy, but seeing no reason to lie.

"And the straw for the hall, the firewood, and the kindling. Is this kept within the courtyard, or without?" went on the leader, gazing fixedly into Jockin's eyes.

Suddenly the jester realized the danger and stopped in his reply. "It is . . ." he began, and then . . . "I do not know."

"I think thou canst remember. . . ." said the man so threateningly that Jockin shivered. But he was saved by a pert voice that piped up, "I know where it is kept, Walter, for I went lately to the kitchen. The kindling and firewood are kept in the outer yard, and also piled in great stacks in the kitchen. The straw is in the stable."

Jockin's eyes were full of dismay, but the leader now stood up and jerked him to his feet.

"Go back to your manor house and forget what you have seen," he ordered. "I'd have left you sleeping forever in the woods, but John-of-the-Field has begged your life, saying you did spare his, and there is one other who is not among us tonight who does also tell that he might have had his ears cropped but for your wit, these three weeks gone. But if one word of this evening's work escapes you, your parents' house shall be burned to the ground that very night, so farewell to you!"

Jockin left the glowing circle as if his feet had wings, but his heart was heavy. Danger was in the air, of what kind, he dared not think, but it threatened all that was dear to him, all that had now become his loyalty and pride.

Now he could guess where his father had refused to go that night and the cause of his mother's anxiety. There was more afoot than man might dare to dream about.

In the morning his adventure seemed a crazy dream, but he knew it had been true.

He went to look at the pear tree in the yard.

It formed a perfect ladder to the top of the wall and he knew children had often used it so. The tree was part of their playground, and they often told how the manor house had been built around it. Sir Richard had a great fancy for the fruit, and Lady Isabel would stew some in sugar syrup and preserve it for the winter, a method that had lately come over from the Continent.

Everyone said how the crooked tree had flourished since the house was built, and soon the wall would have to be pulled down and rebuilt to accommodate its branches.

But now Jockin took an ax from the kitchen, and after a few sharp blows from his brawny arms the pear tree came crashing to the ground.

Squires and pages rushed to the scene at the sound of the ax, followed by maids and ladies-in-waiting, the children of the manor, and the head steward.

"The jester has cut down the pear tree! The jester has cut down the pear tree!" rose on all sides in voices of horror.

The poor tree lay on its side, all dignity, all nobility fled, a mass of broken, tangled branches, where little knotted buds waited so hopefully to bloom. Never again would children's scampering feet run to scramble up the branches. Never again would Philip toss down the juicy fruit to his sisters, nor Lady Isabel take her rare and stately promenade in its shade.

"The jester has cut down the pear tree!" repeated the servants, horrified.

Jockin expected to be flogged, if not flung out of the manor house. He did not realize the license allowed a jester in times of savage punishment and callousness. Nobody raised a hand against him as he faced the steward, trembling and breathing hard.

Sir Richard had heard the noise and appeared in his retiring robe to find the reason for the crash.

"The jester has cut down the pear tree!" he heard on all sides, and there was the tree, it branches spread half across the yard.

"What work is this, fool?" he roared at Jockin, and since he might not speak the truth, the poor boy spoke the first foolish words that came into his head.

"I was plucking a nosegay for the Lady Isabel," he muttered.

It was so much the reply expected of a jester that half the household laughed, and Sir Richard smiled grimly.

"Then you will borrow my sword to pluck a daisy!" he exclaimed, giving Jockin a cuff that was more rough than unkind.

"Clear the courtyard of this half-wit's jest!" he commanded his servants. "At least we shall not have to rebuild the wall."

"If you had played this prank last autumn, I'd not have forgiven you," said Barbara reproachfully, "but Philip is not here, and I shall never, never climb any tree again, for in a few weeks I go to Shrewsbury, to the convent."

The Lady Isabel, who might have been expected to disapprove most strongly of the jester's trick, scarcely mourned the loss of the pear tree. "I had always feared the children would break their legs," she told Father Francis, "and the crawling creatures that dropped upon us in the summer evenings from its branches were most unpleasant. But I fear Philip will be sad."

The dwarf eyed Jockin with great respect, but as if he simply could not understand him.

Chapter 12

The Ride to Shrewsbury

For many a night Jockin lay awake until dawn, listening for the smallest sound that might mean danger for the manor house. He examined every way by which a man might enter unseen, and often strolled around the house before going to bed, chatting with the guards, to satisfy himself that each was in his right place.

He began secretly to teach Ludovic to listen for strangers, for since Sir Richard had found that his hounds were improved, rather than spoiled, by Jockin's training, he allowed the jester to do as he pleased with them, and the great dog was nearly always to be seen following Jockin about, often carrying his bauble in his mouth, which the children thought very funny.

News had come from Edward in Wales that his young brother was pleasing everyone by his good manners and his courage, and the Lady Isabel rose from her bed to take a new interest in the children left to her. There were new dresses to be made for Barbara and chests to be packed with presents for the Abbess at Shrewsbury, for the day was fast approaching when she, too, should leave her home.

As the lovely weeks of early spring succeeded each other, Barbara became more and more unwilling to go and begged her mother to keep her longer at the manor house, but her parents had made up their minds, and the day was already fixed for her journey north to Shrewsbury.

Jockin lost some of his anxiety as the days lengthened and nothing happened to threaten their peace.

The peasants were working as usual on the land. Supplies arrived in the manor kitchen as before. When Jockin visited his home, no strangers knocked, and he saw no strange fires burning outside Lob's hut.

Spring brought hope and cheer to the whole countryside, and Jockin hoped the serfs had forgotten their grievances.

One day in the kitchen he came face to face with the leader of the band that had questioned him in the forest. They recognized each other but spoke no word.

But the man turned to one of the cooks. "And will the fruit harvest be good?" he asked him loudly.

"I cannot say. You should know more of it than I, since we have no fruit trees in the manor house," replied the cook. "And as for our pear tree, this poor fool of a jester chopped it down to make a nosegay for the Lady Isabel!"

At once the man's eyes pierced Jockin like twin arrows. "Have you betrayed us?" they said.

Jockin met his glance without flinching, and the man seemed satisfied. He merely scowled and turned away, seeming so unmoved that Jockin thought the plan, if any, must indeed have been abandoned.

For a week or two he had fears for the safety of his parents' house, but when a fortnight later his father arrived at the manor on some errand, he knew all must be well, and was much relieved.

"Can Jockin ride with us to Shrewsbury?" Barbara plagued her father when Easter drew near.

It was the habit of the lord of the manor to have his jester travel with him, also his pages, his squires, and his men-at-arms, but since Jockin, was less of a buffoon than a household servant, Sir Richard did not often take him along.

"Leave him with us!" Katherine pleaded.

"I want him with me!" Lady Barbara insisted.

"They'll not have him at the convent with you!" Her father laughed. "But if his little white ass will carry him to Shrewsbury, to Shrewsbury he may come."

But after all, it was on a horse and not on the little white donkey that Jockin rode to Shrewsbury the day that Barbara set out. She took leave of her sisters and her mother and received a blessing from Father Francis, then mounted her white palfrey and rode out of the gates at her father's side. Her shining hair had grown again and glinted in the sun. She had forsaken some of her hoydenish ways during the winter and rode like a queen.

It was all comings and goings at the manor, thought Jockin, riding in the procession with a pillion behind his saddle for the dwarf. The dwarf was riding in turn behind the jester and a man-at-arms, and deeply regretted the warm corner in the sunny courtyard where he preferred to spend his days, resting his aged bones.

It was the first time Jockin had journeyed farther from his home than the manor house. He had vaguely believed the forest went on forever, with small patches of fields where men might grow their corn.

But northward stretched the rolling hills and wide acres of untilled country. From time to time they glimpsed a river so wide Jockin could not think how men might cross it or horses swim it. Yet it was not so very wide, the Severn, and the Shropshire hills were more bleak than high. The late March winds blustered down the valleys, and the dwarf shivered, clinging to Jockin's saddle.

Barbara sniffed the air as if she enjoyed it. "I would we were riding on to Wales," she said.

They passed the first night at a hostel on the way, and here Jockin slept outside the Lady Barbara's door, with the dwarf snoring opposite outside the room where slept Sir Richard.

The second night it was the same, only at another hostel, and the dwarf complained till dawn of his aching bones after the long ride.

Jockin lent him his cloak to relieve his sufferings, but he, too, was stiff with the unaccustomed exercise, and between the dwarf's groans and his own aches and pains he slept very little.

The next afternoon, on nearing Bridgenorth, they looked down on the Severn from the top of the hill.

"Let us rest a while down there beside the water," Barbara said to her father, for she was feeling weary, and one more day's riding would see their journey ended. So the whole company plunged down to the greensward beside the river, and sat thankfully beneath the willows to rest, in a brief moment of sunshine.

It was Jockin's duty to entertain his lord while he rested, but he was glad to see Sir Richard had closed his eyes and was snoring as loudly as his dwarf, who had cushioned his head on a saddle and already forgotten his troubles.

Barbara and two or three maids who had ridden with her wandered to the brink of the river to dabble their hands in the water and reach for early kingcups. The flowers eluded them in the most tantalizing manner, and Jockin muddied his red-and-yellow knees kneeling on the bank to fish for them with his bauble, while the bells on his sleeves dipped into the water and the girls shrieked and laughed, imploring him not to drown himself.

But the current washed the stems of the flowers even farther from his reach, and in their anxiety to capture them the girls did not notice an old crone who came limping along the bank with a pitcher in her hand and who, when she reached the merry party, stepped straight into the river without any hesitation and plucked a handful of kingcups, with the water swirling around her waist.

Hoisting herself out of the river, she presented them with a toothless grin to the Lady Barbara, who put out her hand, half recoiling at the old hag and her filthy, sopping rags.

Giving the kingcups to Jockin to hold, Barbara fumbled at her waist for a little silver purse and gave the old woman a coin. Then she wandered toward the horses, Jockin in attendance.

But the other girls lingered, and by their giggles and cries, it became apparent that something was entertaining them greatly. The old woman was still in the center of them, and seemed to be telling their fortunes. Barbara could not resist this novelty. With a great air of dignity she turned to join them, and Jockin, still carrying the flowers, went too.

The girls received their lady with great excitement and some coyness. The old dame had told Bess she was to run into danger and be rescued by a handsome youth, who would become her sweetheart.

Edda was already in love, said the crone, and the other girls clapped their hands, for Edda's romance with one of the foresters was known all over the manor house.

"Tell me my future!" Barbara demanded, hoping that the ragged old woman would not want to take her by the hand. But she merely asked her to hold a little willow branch, which she studied intently after Barbara had handed it back again.

"You are on a journey far from your home," the old crone began. "But you are not so far as you imagine.

Within a week you will be in your mother's arms again."

"No!" cried Barbara, incredulous. "Why, I am on my way to the Benedictine Abbey at Shrewsbury, and I shall stay there three years, until I am married!"

"No convent shall provide your roof this many a day!" said the old woman, shaking her head. "You are unwilling enough to enter, but within three months you will be praying for a peasant's hovel to shelter your head."

"It isn't true! My father has a new and splendid house!" retorted Barbara, thinking that the old hag was repaying her for recoiling at her gift, and also, perhaps, reproaching her for her past misbehavior, knowing she was not worthy to enter a convent. But Father Francis had confessed her, and she had determined to be good and noble-minded forever afterward. What right had this old woman to dash her hopes?

"Aye, new and splendid his house may be today, but what of tomorrow?" said the crone, mumbling and shaking her head. She would tell no more to Barbara.

Embarrassed at seeing their mistress cast down, and a little elated by having a brighter fortune told them than hers, the maids tried to distract her.

"Tell the jester's fortune!" they clamored, clinging around Jockin. "Take the willow wand, good Jester, and hear what the future holds for thee!"

Jockin took the willow wand, which the crone immediately held out to him, and then gave it back.

"You shall render great service to a noble house!" the old woman said. "But first thou shalt cause it great sorrow, and suffer greatly for it thyself."

"Go away, old crone!" Barbara cried angrily, losing her temper. "Why do you threaten us? Even Bess is to meet danger, and I like not your miserable warnings. My father thinks ill of such imaginings."

The maids put their heads together, and the words "witch" were audible. The old crone blanched, and began to retreat, clutching her rags about her.

As the girls still eyed her resentfully, she turned and scurried into the bushes and reeds that hemmed the river.

"Shall we persuade my lord to send the men-at-arms after her?" Barbara asked, turning to Jockin, for she often asked his advice.

"Nay, let her go, she did us no real harm," replied the jester, but he, too, was troubled in spite of himself, for a wise woman had been his mother's earliest guide, and everyone in the forest believed in the wisdom of these people.

The first degree of light went out of the spring afternoon; deeper gold painted the meadow. Mounting their horses, they jingled on to Bridgenorth to spend the night.

Late the following day found them in Shrewsbury, with dusk and a light rain falling. The streets were empty, and the party clattered up the cobbles, eagerly looking forward to the shelter and hospitality for which the convent was famous.

But the great outer door was closed, and though they clanged and clanged again at the big bell, no one opened for them.

Chilly in the rain, the riders huddled under their cloaks, and Barbara wished heartily that she had agreed to ride in the litter, which was the recognized method of traveling for ladies of the day; in fact, her mother had protested strongly, saying that the Abbess would be shocked to see her mounted almost like a man, but Sir Richard took her part, saying the litter slowed up the pace of the party, which did not please him or his daughter at all.

But the litter would have been a haven this chill evening, and Barbara fidgeted uneasily on her damp palfrey, finally bidding Jockin go look around and see if there was not some other way to enter the convent.

Jockin turned his horse aside down a narrow street bounded by the high convent wall and presently saw a lad approaching at the far end of the street with a large rush basket. He stopped below a small window in the wall and made some sign or sound, for, to Jockin's surprise, a cord was let down and attached to the basket, which was then hauled up and taken inside. The lad turned on his heel and hurried away whistling.

Urging his tired nag up the street, Jockin was in time to see a black-clad nun closing the unglazed window through which the basket had disappeared.

He hailed her.

"Holy Sister! Sir Richard is here, awaiting the pleasure of your Lady Abbess. He waits without, and no one opens the door!"

The nun turned a face of terror to him. "No one may come in or out! The Death has returned to us. The Lady Abbess lies sick, but we think she will recover. Five of the sisters are stricken, and one is already dead."

New to the horror of the returning plague that had struck him once and was to strike the land in spasmodic bursts during the next fifty years, Jockin quailed within, and rode back to his lord with a heart full of foreboding.

But at last the door had been opened and the same news related to Sir Richard by an aged sister who had overcome the sickness the year before. She repeated the dreadful news and advised Sir Richard to find accommodation in the town, and then to take his daughter home.

But Sir Richard would not risk his daughter's life in

a town which he felt sure was infested by the return of the terrible Black Death. Weary as they all were, chilled and drenched with the spring rain, they turned and hastened out of the city at the best pace the horses could make, riding all night with very few stops till they came to Bridgenorth.

The party was in sad straits when they arrived. Horses were lame and riders weary.

The Lady Barbara, half dead with fatigue, only remained in her saddle through pride and the fear of the sickness behind her. Jockin told her stories to help the wearisome journey, while the wretched maids, riding pillion behind menservants sobbed and listened and listened and sobbed in turn.

When at last they reached the hostel, they were all too weary to eat but slept late into the next day and awoke fearful that even now the sickness might overtake them.

But Bridgenorth was free of the sickness and so, rested and refreshed, they set off again for home and reached it exactly one week after their setting out. Glad enough was Barbara, and Jockin too, to see the gates of the manor house again, and glad enough was Lady Isabel to have her daughter back again after such a dreadful exposure to danger.

Chapter 13

A Bundle of Straw

So Barbara got her wish, and was not at once sent to the convent but passed the summer months in her beloved home, with Jockin to amuse her, and all that made life pleasant and tolerable continuing as before.

Rides and picnics in the forest, small jousts to prove the squires, pageants, the comings and goings of guests and relatives, day after day passed like a string of bright beads down a thread, till Jockin's boyhood fell behind him like an old cloak and his place in the manor house was never more secure.

He was so much in demand these days that he seldom visited his home, but when he could not go to them, his parents walked the long miles to the manor house kitchen, where he received them joyfully and saw to it that the cook did not send them away empty-handed.

There were few among the servants who were not Jockin's friends, and the cook was one of the most loyal. He boasted about their son to Plow Jockin and his wife till their eyes shone with dumb pride, and they stumbled home happy to have bred such a hero.

But there remained one or two who were indifferent to him, while the dwarf was always spiteful and unfriendly, knowing that his own place was lost forever the day Jockin came to the manor. Another enemy was one of the grooms, a lazy fellow always in trouble with Sir Richard, who bore a grudge against Jockin for the care he lavished on Lady Barbara's palfrey, hitherto his own neglected charge.

128

This man was often in the kitchen, hanging around for scraps or gossiping with those who came in from forest and village, instead of doing his own work in the stable. Once Jockin saw him whispering into the ear of that man who had certainly been the leader of the band at Lob's hut, and when he saw Jockin they separated and went their different ways.

When harvest came, there was more complaining in the great hall of the difficulty of getting laborers for the reaping, and once more Sir Richard vowed he would not bribe them. The shadow of danger that had threatened in the winter threatened again. Jockin felt spying eyes everywhere and was glad he had cut down the pear tree.

One lovely summer evening Jockin met Jack, the groom, crossing the courtyard with a truss of straw under his arm. The man staggered and sweated as if he had been working hard. His breath came in short gasps, and he stumbled with the truss as though it weighed as much as a sack of wheat.

Such harmony and beauty were in the air that Jockin forgot the man's unfriendliness, and kindly offered to help with the load, though it crossed his mind that a truss of straw would make few men sweat, unless they were as little used to work as poor Jack.

To his surprise, the only answer he got as he stooped to lift the truss was a kick on the shins that tripped him up and sent him flying on the cobbles.

It was a common enough sport to make the jester tumble unexpectedly—in fact, he usually landed on his hands with his legs in the air—but this time the blow was given with such fury and deliberation that Jockin remained prostrate with bewilderment, watching the retreating figure of Jack struggling around the stable door with the burden that had caused him so much trouble.

"Why do you sit thus, Jester?" asked young Francis curiously, coming to his side.

"I have been seeking the roundest cobble in the yard, so now I sit upon it, to keep it warm," replied Jockin, in the language he knew was expected of him and which he was at last beginning to learn. The Lady Barbara implored him nowadays, "Never practice these common jests upon me, but speak me true!" But Francis, who had been brought up more conventionally, expected no more and asked no further questions.

It was in Jockin's mind to follow Jack to the stables and examine the history of the bundle of straw, but when he remembered the bitterly angry expression on the man's face, he guessed it would be more prudent to wait.

He therefore settled himself, in the last rays of the setting sun, opposite the stable door and at a long distance from it, chewing a feather, and whistling to a blackbird who was chanting his vespers above in Lady Isabel's garden.

Father Francis found him here and stopped, as he often did, to speak with him.

"Ah, my son, now you sing as blithely as the blackbird itself! But it was as a caged bird that you came to me, these eleven months back, to mourn your freedom. You have soon learned how to turn your complaining into contentment."

"Aye, Father!" Jockin replied, bowing his head before the kindly priest. "Indeed, I am now content to serve my lord. But I might not have been, had you not shown me the way."

"The manor house is brighter for your coming," said Father Francis. "Every man has this power to make his fellows better or worse by his presence. You use your gifts well. Give the praise to God who put you in this world."

He passed out of sight and young Francis loitered by again.

"Now you look joyful, as if you had received great news," he said enviously. "What did Father Francis tell you? He never tells me anything but dull, dry Latin and Greek. I care for him not. I would I were home in Wales!"

This was his usual cry, and often tears followed.

The petted, spoiled boy, still missing his mother's caresses and finding no substitute in his cold, unbending Aunt Isabel, either could not or would not settle down to his new life, made no friends, and was teased unmercifully by the other pages and by his cousin Barbara. Like her, but for a different reason, he clung to Jockin, yet despised him, because he was only a poor jester.

To distract him and curb the quivering lip, Jockin said, "It comes to me that the little Lady Isabel left her silver whip in the stables this morning. I saw it lying in her pony's stall." Francis strolled halfheartedly across the courtyard, but returned almost immediately without the whip, looking startled and angry.

"Jack said it was not there, and ordered me out!" he exclaimed with indignation. "He says my Lord Richard's horse is sick and must not be affrighted. But there he stands talking to a strange man and naught wrong with the horse that I can see. He eats well enough!"

The strange conduct of Jack caused Jockin to knit his brows and chew furiously on the feather he held between his teeth. He determined not to leave his post until Jack appeared again, but barely twenty minutes had gone by before sounds of woe arose from within the manor house, the children crying and wailing and calling his name in a manner that could not be disregarded.

"Oh, Jockin! Come quickly! Ludo! Ludo!"

"Ludo has been poisoned!" cried little Katherine, rushing out to the courtyard and flinging herself weeping into the jester's arms.

Jockin followed her into the great hall, where Barbara sat sorrowing over the body of her father's great hound.

True enough, poor Ludovic, their friend and playmate, Sir Richard's favorite dog of the chase, lay stretched dead in front of the dais where he had so often lain at his master's feet.

Jockin fondled the head of his old friend and shed tears with the children.

The household was shocked, and Sir Richard furious. The dog had been at his heels all day and had traveled some miles from home. He might have picked up poison anywhere. Some peasant, perhaps, had poisoned food scraps to destroy wild animals around his home.

Three of the servants were sent to dig his grave in the forest under the trees where he had so often hunted. Jockin went with them to see the last of his old friend, and they walked some little way into the woods, with the summer dusk caressing them like a soft, deep blanket waiting to enfold them.

The three men from the manor house babbled ceaselessly, speaking of their own affairs, but Jockin was silent, thinking partly of Ludovic and partly of the sinister atmosphere that seemed to surround the manor this evening even more certainly than the dusk. He kept a sharp lookout to right and left, his country senses by no means dulled by the year in Sir Richard's service, but there was nothing to be seen. Rather, the woods seemed less full of warning than the house.

Their sorrowful work over, the four of them returned, with the pleasure of the evening meal before them, but Jockin, excused from his lord's table (Sir Richard had finished dining when he returned), uneasy, and suspicious, went directly to the courtyard and then to the stables looking for Jack.

He found him there, sitting on a log, and apparently on guard over Sir Richard's horse, who had not any appearance of being ill, but was eating hungrily, throwing up its head to whinny as Jockin came in.

Of the bundle of straw or the stranger that young Francis had mentioned there was no sign.

Jack scowled darkly as the jester entered.

"My lord's horse is sick?" Jockin asked. All the animals were so devoted to him, and he cared for them so constantly that none could be surprised at his asking.

"He ails," replied the man shortly.

"Has the horse doctor been here to see him? The pages tell me they saw a stranger talk with thee," said the jester boldly.

Jack the groom flushed dark red.

"The horse doctor came," he muttered.

"Did he name the sickness?" Jockin asked.

"He knew not what it could be."

"Mayhap he, too, is poisoned, like poor Ludovic," said Jockin. "Yet not like Ludo, for poor Ludo is dead, while Altar is like to get well, if he does eat so well as now."

The angry groom seemed as if he would spring at Jockin and knock him down, only the jester had had the wit to place himself on the far side of the horse, who, being nervous, would certainly flash out his heels at any sudden movement on the part of Jack, the groom, and when Jockin had cast his eyes all around the stable in vain search for any suspicious object or person, he strolled casually out of the door and back to the manor hall.

Chapter 14

The Burning of the Manor House

The dwarf was in excellent spirits that night, for the dog Ludovic had been his greatest enemy.

It is only fair to say that the dwarf had been at a disadvantage with the great hound, who in his puppy days had bowled poor Dobbin over like a top in his play, teasing him with his rough tongue and playful licks and seeming to take mischievous pleasure in bouncing out at him from behind an arras, or barking his deep, terrifying bark right in his victim's ear. In revenge, the dwarf had tormented the dog till each hated the sight of the other, and Ludovic growled menacingly whenever the dwarf appeared.

Even Sir Richard believed, at first, that the dwarf had given the poison to the dog, but Lady Isabel pointed out that he had not left her side all the day, while Ludovic had been with his master. Also, it was a well-known fact that the hound would not accept any food from the dwarf's hand, nor from any vessel that had been handled by him.

So, his innocence established, the dwarf rejoiced, and chanted his joy to mock at Jockin when they lay in their own corners that night.

"No more bears' tricks for thee, poor Jester, thy best pupil is no more!" he gloated.

Jockin took no notice. Trying to keep himself awake, he was listening with both ears to the night sounds of the house—Sir Richard snoring in his bed, the wind sighing around the corners, one of the squires babbling suddenly in his sleep, and a muffled whinny from Altar in the stable.

He missed Ludovic's deep growl, which sometimes pierced the night when some strange sound fell on the dog's keen ear. But poor Ludovic would growl no more. He slept quietly forever under the pine trees in the forest.

Thinking affectionately of his old friend, Jockin fell asleep. He dreamed he was a prisoner again among a crowd of peasants, some known to him and some unknown. Once more they had dragged him with them to old Lob's hut, where a roaring fire lit up their faces and drowned their excited voices.

He awoke suddenly to hear the roaring and crackling still in his ears, voices loud in the hall below, cries, shouts and, farther away, someone calling for Sir Richard.

As he struggled to his elbow on his hard shelf, Jockin saw a scarlet, flickering glow reflected on the opposite wall. The narrow, winding stairs leading from the family's private apartments to the hall glowed as if someone had hung a fiery tapestry upon them. The dark lump outside Sir Richard's door that was the dwarf was brightly outlined in the glow, and flung a shadow as in daylight.

In the hall, voices screamed and shouted.

Jockin sprang to his feet.

At the same moment Sir Richard in his nightclothes appeared at his door, while up the stair in wild and disordered habit bounded the priest, closely followed by Sir Richard's steward, who gave the dwarf a great shove that roused him properly.

"The house is afire, my lord!" the steward gasped. "The people have set it alight! There is straw blazing behind the arras in the hall and they have thrown lighted bundles dipped in pitch over the wall into the courtyard. They are threatening you and all your family, my lord, and the watchmen cannot hold the gate for long. Besides, the house burns fast, and the well is deep. We cannot draw water fast enough to put it out."

Father Francis had not stopped, but bounded up the farther flight of stairs to the room occupied by the nurse and the two little girls. Jockin was beside him—they pulled the children from their covers, flung wraps around them, and roused the sleeping nurse, who began immediately to scream, while the children whimpered piteously.

"Take your charge!" Father Francis sternly bade her, pushing the bundle that was little Isabel into the woman's arms. "Bring such clothes as you can find, good Jester, and follow me below."

Carrying Katherine, the priest disappeared down the narrow stairway, closely followed by the frightened nurse.

Jockin snatched an armful of clothes and bedspreads and hurried after them, meeting the white-faced Lady Isabel on the landing, wringing her hands and begging her husband to have all the peasants hanged who had taken part in such a deed.

The dwarf gibbered at her heels, terrified of the fire and of no use to his mistress. Sir Richard had already gone below.

Jockin escorted his lady and the shivering dwarf to the hall, the farther end of which was well alight, while the fire, creeping along the arrases, gained terrible hold even as they watched it.

Already the glazed windows, pride of Sir Richard's heart, were cracking in the heat, and Jockin could see that in a very short time the roof would fall in.

Sir Richard saw the danger too, and crowded the whole

party back into the anteroom between the kitchen and the hall.

But beyond the kitchen door new arrows of light flickered and crackled. A second outburst of fire had certainly broken out in that spot, and above the noise of the fire came hoarse cries and shouts from without that were not the cries of rescuers, but threatening and dangerous.

"They mean to roast us alive!" said Sir Richard, looking grimly at his wife and children. "Where is the Lady Barbara?"

Jockin had already discovered that Barbara was not with them, and even before his lord had spoken he had bounded back up the stairs.

The air was hot and stifling now, full of smoke and sparks.

As he climbed the stairs, a roar behind him told of the collapse of one of the great beams in the hall, and the leaping flames that followed lighted the whole twisted length of the flight, giving out such a heat that he felt his back hot with it. Never had he believed that fire could make such an uproar. It was as if an enormous dragon had been unleashed in the manor hall and was plunging around between the walls, laying waste to all that it sprang upon. Jockin's heart hammered loud with fear, but his thoughts were for his lady.

He knocked loudly on Barbara's door, and to his surprise she opened it directly. She was ready dressed and looked at him calmly.

"I heard the steward's words," she said, "and I was about to join my mother, when methought it were more convenient to dress myself."

You had waited almost too long! thought Jockin, but aloud he said, catching her hand, "Quickly, my lady,

quickly! The hall is all alight and I know not when the
roof may fall. We must run fast to join the others before
we are cut off!"

The heavy oak door of her room had muffled the noise
of the raging fire. Barbara had thought to make her
descent with dignity, but at the top of the stairs she
blanched, clutching at Jockin's hand. "What is that terrible noise? Who is shouting so outside? Those are not
the voices of our servants!"

"Hurry, hurry!" Jockin urged, pulling her after him,
though what safety lay below he had not stopped to think,
and at that very moment with a tremendous roar the
roof of the hall fell in below, sending up coils of smoke
and ash that reached up the stairs in choking clouds,
blinding and stifling them both.

When they had cleared their lungs and streaming eyes,
nothing could be heard but the fearful burning of the
fire, which was drawn up through the gutted walls of the
hall as if it had been a chimney.

"Let's go down quickly!" Barbara cried.

Jockin led the way, but the heat was unbearable; soon
he had to stop.

"Go on!" Barbara cried, gasping, a few steps behind him.

Jockin held his breath and turned the last corner of
the stairs, but the burning debris of the roof filled the
hall, and already the flames were hungry again and reaching for the stairs.

Pushing Barbara backward, Jockin turned and rushed
with her up the stairs again. Coughing and panting, she
did not try to protest. It was only too plain that the hall
was beyond their hopes.

"We can never reach the rest," Jockin said. "Let us go
out to Lady Isabel's roof garden."

Lady Isabel's apartments seemed a haven, her little roof

garden a paradise of cool, sweet air, a different world from the raging terror below.

Jockin and Barbara leaned on the terrace, filling their scorched lungs as if they could not have too much of it. The quiet, too, was blissful, and the cool night air a balm.

In the distance they could still hear the angry shouts of the peasants outside.

"They call for my father!" Barbara said. "Oh, how could they treat him thus!"

If my lord will not bargain with them, he will lose more than his manor, Jockin thought, but aloud he said, "They are angry, and we had best avoid them. Do you remember, my lady, that Philip used to drop from this garden to the lower terrace and thence over the outer wall to the world outside?"

"Aye, and so I did when I was young!" said Barbara, with an impish smile that suddenly gave place to a look of horror as she cried, "Philip! And he prayed me care for his monkey while he was away! It sleeps in the press in my room! Fetch him quickly, Jockin, before the fire reaches him, or Philip will never, never pardon me!"

Jockin flew back through Lady Isabel's apartments and found all the rooms full of smoke. Flames were licking the walls of the stairs; he could see they had escaped with little or no time to spare. The noise of burning below was terrible.

He found the little monkey crouching in the press in his lady's room, whimpering with terror, for animals are quick to recognize their primitive enemy—fire—and the poor creature clung to Jockin like a child. It would not leave him to go to Barbara, and the jester was forced to help her to the top of the wall with the monkey's arms wound tightly around his neck.

Barbara spurned Jockin's hands, dropping to the next terrace like a boy, with a torn dress to mark her passage. Jockin dropped lightly after her. Together they ran the length of the terrace and down a flight of steps that led toward the kitchen premises.

Here the shouting and threatening of the mob was loudest; it sounded as though some had already forced their way into the small courtyard that bounded on the kitchen, and their demands for Sir Richard were loud and insistent.

Jockin bade Barbara wait, and cautiously opened the small door leading from the terrace to the courtyard. He poked his head around the corner to see what might be happening.

The whole scene was bright as daylight with the light of the flames. The storerooms and watchhouses of the north side of the manor were on fire, and the watchmen had evidently been overcome, for the rebellious peasants had surged into the yard and were pressing and hammering on the door that led to the kitchen apartments.

It was no place to take his lady, and Jockin was about to close the door quietly again when he saw a very small child, no more than a baby, sitting on the cobbles, as if it had tried to creep away from the tumult and terror, but had been balked by the closed door.

Jockin snatched it up and was back with Lady Barbara in an instant, but hardly had he bolted the door behind him than someone began to batter and pummel at it, while an anxious voice called his name in great fear from the far side.

With the baby under one arm and the monkey on his shoulder, the jester pulled the bolt and opened the door a chink.

"Jockin! It is I! Let me through!" implored a piteous voice, and young Francis, the page, slipped through beside them. He was trembling and disheveled, his fair hair tumbling about his eyes, which were so full of terror that the jester put a comforting arm around his shoulders.

"I tried to escape, and the crowd drove me back! They wish to kill my Uncle Richard!" Francis gasped.

Barbara gave a little scream. "They would not dare!" she exclaimed passionately. "Let me get to my father! Open the door, Jockin, else I will reach him by the way we came!"

But at that moment a shout arose from the courtyard and fierce hands battled with the door. The escape of Francis had been seen, and taking it for another entrance to the manor, the angry peasants began to storm it.

"Quickly! We must escape by the wall!" said Jockin. "We can do nothing for my Lord Richard by staying here. Up the steps, Sir Francis, and onto the wall where it is shallowest. Then hang by your hands and drop. It is a long fall, but it is simple if you bend your knees. Then be ready to break the fall of your lady cousin whom I will let down to you."

"Put down the baby and come quickly!" cried Barbara, alive to the danger threatening even more loudly from without.

Francis ran ahead, peering timidly over the high wall to the ground below.

"We shall break our limbs," he whimpered.

"Nay, Philip and I did but graze our knees each time we did so!" said his cousin scornfully. "See how it is done!"

Before Jockin, hampered by the baby, could stop her, Barbara had slipped lightly over the wall. Hanging for one moment by her hands, she dropped like a cat, staggered a little, and stood looking up at them, triumphant, but her face was set as if in pain.

"Are you hurt, my lady?" Jockin cried anxiously, peering

down at her from where he and Francis stood on the wall.

Shaded from the firelight, the ground seemed dark and mysterious. Barbara's face peered up like a pale moon out of the shadows.

"I did but twist my foot a little. Come quickly!" she replied impatiently.

"Go you next, and remember to bend well at the knee on landing," the jester said, giving Francis a little push.

"I dare not! I dare not!" the boy wept. "I shall break my legs—it is so far to fall and I am weak. I am not like my cousin Barbara, who is more a man than a maid!"

"I am not!" shouted his indignant cousin, furious at this insult to her long-labored-at dignity and manners. "But if he will not come, good Jockin, do you come yourself and leave him, the great crybaby, to dry his tears at the flames. Come quickly, Jockin!"

Jockin, however, soothed the trembling boy and finally persuaded him to climb on the wall. Then, putting the monkey and the baby on the terrace at his feet for a moment, he took the page's wrists and held him at arm's length over the other side of the wall.

"When I say drop, flex your limbs!" he commanded him.

Francis obeyed with a pitiful little wail, landing at his cousin's feet with no worse damage than badly grazed knees.

"Now you, good Jockin! Follow us quickly!" Barbara called, but Jockin was looking for something in which he could lower the baby. He did not think of leaving it behind.

Between the fire and the feet of the angry mob, the poor little creature, whoever it was, could hardly hope to survive, and he handled it with the same care and tenderness he offered Baby Isabel, though by its poor dress it was quite evidently a servant's child.

"Come quickly!" Barbara called in a fever of impatience, while from the noises at the foot of the steps it appeared the crowd was attacking the door with some kind of a post or pole.

Jockin saw nothing that would help him, while above, the flames flickered high in the Lady Isabel's room.

"Leave the child! Someone will find it!" cried Barbara, as she saw him put one leg over the wall, the child on his arm.

"It is the washerwoman's baby," added Francis, as concerned as Barbara at the jester's madness.

With the monkey clinging on the back of his neck and the baby wailing under one arm, Jockin lowered himself by the other till he hung by one hand only to the top of the wall. His acrobatics stood him in good stead, and his sturdy muscles bore his weight with ease once the first wrench was over, but the boy and girl below waited in agony for the drop that might end in disaster.

It came, and Jockin dropped.

Though the weight of the child upset his balance and he rolled over on landing, no harm was done. The baby was not even scratched and the monkey sprang nimbly to the ground as Jockin fell.

Even as they crouched below the wall they heard the door give way.

A dozen men rushed up to the terrace shouting angrily, and they felt rather than saw the faces that peered over the wall. But thanks to the darkness nobody noticed them at all.

When they realized that the terrace did not lead them into the house, the peasants ran back to the courtyard, and the little party began to creep cautiously forward under the wall, in the opposite direction to the noise and shouting.

Suddenly a great clatter of hooves approached, and three or four horses, wild with fear or excitement, nearly swept them off their feet, galloping around the corner of the house as if sparks were in their feet.

"Oh, I am glad they have escaped the fire!" cried Barbara thankfully. "There goes Altar, and there my lovely Melisande! How they fly and how terrified their eyes are! They will never stop galloping till morning!"

"If we had known they were coming, we might have stopped them!" said Jockin anxiously. "A horse might mean safety for us now."

"Then your wish is granted, Sir Jester!" said Barbara, laughing hysterically, for around the corner of the house trotted the little white donkey.

Jockin snatched at its head before the frightened animal could break away, and with the thong around his waist made a passable halter.

Then, still carrying the baby in his arms and with the monkey again on his shoulders, the jester led his little party away from the burning manor, skirting the village green and avoiding the houses, though they were almost certainly empty, with everyone at the scene of the fire.

He invited Barbara to ride, but though her ankle pained her, she was too proud, so it was Francis who rested his sore knees and carried the baby in front of him on his bony perch.

Leaving the bright light behind them illuminating the village and trees for a great distance around, Jockin plunged into the woods where the shadows were deepest, and so, stumbling and blinded, they pushed on to find a hiding place for the rest of the night.

Chapter 15

The Escape to the Forest

When the weary children could go no farther, Jockin tied the donkey to a tree and saw Barbara and Francis tumble asleep on the ground. The washerwoman's baby had long since fallen asleep, and he laid it gently under a tree wrapped in his own hood.

The jester sat for a long while watching over his charges, his brow puckered with bewilderment and care.

What was he to do? How was he to care for these poor children if their home, as appeared likely, had really been burned to the ground?

And if Sir Richard and the rest of his family had actually been destroyed, would his daughter and his nephew be safe in the woods, with the peasants in revolt, and every hand raised against the lords of the manor?

He thought at once of his mother. She would cherish the poor, innocent baby, and offer shelter to the Lady Barbara as she had done before. Young Francis, too, would be safe in the cottage, but Jockin remembered the threats made to him in the forest by old Lob's hut. Might he not bring equal disaster on his parents' house by associating with it? The poor fellow tore his hair and chewed at the points of his motley in his self-questioning—what was best to do?

One thing was certain: he had to find out how things were at the manor house, whether the walls still stood, whether the fire had been quenched (he had seen no attempt of any kind to put it out), whether Sir Richard had

145

succeeded in overcoming the peasants, or whether they had overcome him. Such a fearful thought made Jockin tremble, but with the common people in such a temper as he had witnessed, he could believe almost anything.

The glade where the children lay was deeply hidden, cool and shadowy even by day. The coat of the little white donkey gleamed dully. Jockin led it away behind a bush, tying up its jaws with Barbara's silken scarf that it might not bray. The monkey slept, shivering a little, at the foot of a tree.

Then he looked again at the children, unwilling to leave them without a sign.

As if she felt his perplexity, Barbara suddenly sat up on her elbow. "Jockin!" she cried.

"Listen, my lady!" Jockin dropped on one knee at her side. "I go to see what is forward at the manor house."

"I will go with you!" Barbara cried eagerly.

"Nay, my lady, let me first perceive if it is safe and how things may stand for our return. Do you stay here with your cousin and the child till I come back and bring the news. If the child should cry, here is a lump of sweet stuff, give it this to suck."

"I cannot think why you brought the brat!" grumbled Barbara angrily, looking at the sleeping child. "Will you not take it with you?"

"Nay, I will not," said Jockin shortly, and she knew it was useless to protest.

"Delay not in your coming!" she ordered as he stood up. "And bring us bread or cakes! I am starving with hunger. Tell my father I am safe, and if you can catch my palfrey, bring it here to me. Francis can ride the donkey." She lay back on the moss, while Jockin set off catfoot through the woods by the way they had come.

The gray dawnlight had only begun to pierce the trees,

but morning was coming. Jockin trod carefully when he approached the village, slipping in and out of the trees like a wood deer, afraid his bright garments would betray him, but until the sun rose, everything was either light or shade, and even the gaunt, smoking ruins of the manor had lost the terrible splendor painted by the flames.

The crumbling walls smoked furiously, pockets of scarlet ash appeared here and there, while charred window frames hung distorted from their arches. Sections still collapsed, smoldering; small flames flickered and subsided; but there was no heart and no life left in the manor house that had been the pride of Sir Richard's heart; it was a hopeless ruin, and even the spectators and those who had wantonly ruined it had crept away.

Jockin was struck by a terrible grief. Forgetting all caution, he crept out of the trees, crossed the village green, and walked around the house. Smoldering and hot, there was no entry anywhere.

The stables had collapsed; he was glad he had seen the horses freed. The wall over which they had escaped was blackened and partly sagging, the stones were warm to his touch.

There was no sign of life, and it was hopeless to expect that anyone still lived in that smoking shell that had been the Lady Barbara's home.

When he had walked twice around the manor, he ran back to the woods, for every moment brought the sunrise nearer and he did not want to be seen.

Yet he longed to ask someone what had been the end of the terrible burning, and whether the rest of the family had escaped, and if so, whither they had fled.

He walked a few paces up the road they had taken that long-ago spring day when they set out for Shrewsbury.

Would that the plague had not then ended our mission!

Would that my Lady Barbara were safe in her priory now! thought the jester, trying to find traces of footprints in the dust in the half-light.

He had hardly turned the first bend in the road before there came a clatter of hooves behind him, so sudden and clear at that early hour that Jockin jumped hurriedly behind a tree, peeping out to see who came so suddenly and at such a pace.

To his great surprise, he saw the dwarf on his little pony, which, when the jester hailed his master, stood up on its hind legs in surprise, nearly throwing its rider in the road.

Between terror and rage, the dwarf fairly chattered his teeth when he saw Jockin step out from behind his tree.

"Would you break my neck, fool?" he snarled angrily, jerking the pony's head away from the jester's hand.

"Nay, if you will not burn, you will not break!" replied Jockin. "Tell me the news quick, Sir Dwarf. How goes it with my lord, and Lady Isabel? Are the children safe?"

"My lord is well, my lady too; the children are safe and all the household, save only my Lady Barbara and one of the pages. 'Tis thought she perished in her room, being slow to join the rest before the roof fell in. 'Twas thought you did perish with her, young Jockin, being sent to find her, but I see now thou art too little of a fool to singe thy motley. My congratulations, Sir Jester!"

"And Sir Richard! Where is he now?" cried Jockin anxiously.

"He is rode away with all the household. My lady and the children travel in a charred litter!" said the dwarf. "They are but an hour on the road ahead of me. It took half the night to round up the horses, and my pony had run the farthest. I have been this while pursuing him and now I do follow them hard. Keep me not, Sir Jester!"

"And the peasants, did they let them by?" Jockin asked anxiously.

"Aye, they stopped them not. Sullen they were, but they did no more harm. At least they fear my Lord Richard," said the dwarf, not without satisfaction. "And with the Lady Barbara's death on their hands they have good cause, for my lord will never rest till he has hanged 'em all!"

"The Lady Barbara is not dead. I have her safely in the forest," said Jockin. "Do you ride on, good Dwarf, and tell my lord that we come. Pray him to wait for us at the first convenient spot, and do you mark the way that we may travel for us to follow you. Young Sir Francis is with us, but footsore and weary, and, too, the young baby of the washerwoman. We have but the little white donkey to carry the four of us. Know you whither my lord will ride?"

The dwarf's eyes, which had opened wide at Jockin's words, now became cunning.

"Nay, I know not," he replied. "They say the whole country is in an uproar. The peasants rise on all sides. Who knows where he may be received, or where it is safe for him to go? You had best tread carefully, Sir Jester, with so great a charge."

"Perhaps, after all, you had best tell my lord I take them to my parents' house!" said Jockin, perplexed.

"Your parents' house!" The dwarf laughed long and unpleasantly. "Why, my poor jester, would you deliver thy poor babes straight to the fire? *Your father was there at the burning!*"

The shock Jockin received on hearing these words paralyzed his limbs. His arms fell useless to his sides. At the same time the dwarf dug his heels into the pony's sides and cantered away up the road laughing a high cruel cackle that tempted Jockin to send a stone flying after him.

"Mark me well the way at the crossroads!" he cried, but whatever reply the dwarf made was lost in the clatter of the pony's hooves.

He had dropped his black woolen cloak, however, and this Jockin picked up and wound hastily around his yellow coat, as he stood looking after the retreating figure, turning his words over and over in his heart.

His father with the rebel peasants that had fired the manor!

For a full half minute Jockin felt tempted to run the long miles to his home to hear from his parents' own lips if this was true, but the thought of the poor children in their hiding place was too urgent for hesitation; they must be awakened and set on their way before the peasants roused themselves to ponder on their night's work or seek new destruction.

If, as the dwarf had said, they were in a rebel temper in all parts, then the sooner the children had safely joined to the household, the better, for a large company traveled more safely than a small one.

Reminded by his own hunger, Jockin called to mind Barbara's plea for cakes or bread. He remembered the dwarf had had quite a large bag hanging on his back, and wondered if he had thought to rob the kitchen before escaping. Certainly there would be nothing fit to eat left in the kitchen now.

Toward the village was a small cottage with a henhouse. The rooster had been crowing for some time, and now a sleepy noise of cackling showed that the hens were stirring. Jockin knew that the cottage dwellers rose early, but he trusted to the night's disturbance to deepen their morning slumbers and crept toward the henhouse like any prowling cat stealing for her young.

The drowsy hens squawked and complained, the rooster flapped and escaped to crow his vengeance in the pen, but before the first noises had subsided, Jockin was running silently through the trees with the eggs wrapped in the dwarf's black cloak, and the pleasant news of breakfast as well as her family's safety to carry to his lady.

She, newly awakened from her second sleep, was delighted to see him.

"Oh, what a long night! And what a pleasant morning! I always wanted to see the sun rise from the woods! Is my father anxious about me, Jockin, and have they put out the fire in the house?"

"The fire still smolders," Jockin said soberly. "The house is burned almost to the ground. There is nothing alive left in it. My Lord Richard and all the household are ridden away. We must follow them immediately."

"Indeed we must!" said Barbara, startled to her feet. "But how came my father to go without me? How could he leave me to sleep in the woods with no one to look after me?"

"He thought you were dead, my lady, burned in the fire last night," said Jockin. "The dwarf, whom I met, told me so."

"Oh, my poor father!" cried Barbara. "Let us follow him quickly. But what did you bring us to eat, my good Jockin, for I am starving to death!"

"I am starving to death also!" complained Francis, raising a woebegone face from the damp moss. "And I am shivering and sore. Why did you bring us into these woods, Jockin, and let my Lord Richard go on without us?"

It was a question poor Jockin found hard to answer,

and when the baby, hearing their voices, awoke and began to cry, he could do nothing but stare at their three accusing faces, wondering how indeed he could have come to use them so ill.

"Jockin could not help it. The stairs were burning and the peasants in the courtyard were like to kill us," said Barbara. "You are a poor fool, Francis, and if Jockin had not dropped you over the wall, you would be burned or trampled to death by now. But give us to eat, good Jockin. I cannot walk nor ride a step until I have crammed myself full. 'Tis sleeping in the woods gives me an appetite."

Jockin could only dumbly hold out the three eggs he had stolen, grubby from the hen's feet in the henhouse. The two children looked at them in disgust. The baby bawled loudly, but the monkey snatched at them.

"What—are they cooked?" Barbara asked, wrinkling her nose.

"Nay, I took them from a henhouse," Jockin said. "There was no bread, no meat, and no meal. The manor is ruined and smoking. No one can enter it."

"Is it true?" Barbara asked, as if she had heard him for the first time. "But what of our villagers? The village is not far away. Rouse them and get us bread, and milk for the poor babe. Fly, Jockin, for we starve, and my father will be expecting us."

"The peasants are in a strange temper," Jockin said, shaking his head. " 'Tis they who did this to my lord's manor. I know not how they may now act against us. My lord is gone. I do not like to make ourselves known to them for fear how they may treat you while they still seek vengeance. I can ask nothing of them."

"Then take me to your parents. 'Tis a long walk, but at least they will give us bread!" said Barbara.

"I dare not," said Jockin with such pain in his voice that Barbara asked no more questions.

"Then I will eat an egg, for eat I must!" she exclaimed, breaking a shell and tipping the contents into her mouth.

Her cousin watched her, shuddering. "How can you do so, Barbara?" he protested, his narrow frame racked with disgust.

Meanwhile Jockin broke a second egg and fed the baby, who showed no surprise at its unusual diet and lapped up the raw egg partly from the shell and partly from Jockin's fingers, as if it could have disposed of a dozen in the same way.

Barbara looked on half admiringly and half in scorn.

"It is a handsome child," she remarked when Jockin had cleaned its face and hands with a corner of his cloak. "But I cannot think what made you bring it with us, Jockin. You had best leave it in the village before we set off."

To her the child of a servant, and the washerwoman at that, was worth no care or trouble, and she marveled to see Jockin soothe and feed it, finally rocking it back to sleep in his arms. It had a few fine teeth, he was glad to see, and seemed rather more than a year old. He was glad it could eat the egg, and the lump of sweet stuff would console it by and by.

"If you will ride now, my lady, the child will sleep in your arms," he said, untying the donkey.

"I will carry it as far as the village," agreed Barbara graciously, mounting the donkey.

But Francis complained. His knees pained him and bled afresh. All his limbs ached and he had not slept a wink all night. He did not think he could walk all the way until they caught up with the household, not without a bite of food inside him.

"There is still an egg," said Jockin, arranging his lady on the donkey.

"I cannot eat it!" complained Francis. "I have no stomach for such fare. Never have I eaten a raw egg. Food for stableboys and washerwomen's children!"

"I will smite your face!" cried Barbara hotly, preparing to dismount and do so, but Jockin and the burden of the baby prevented her, so they left the glade with Francis limping sulkily in the rear and Jockin keeping a careful watch for foresters, peasants, or passersby of any kind. The monkey rode on his shoulder.

The foresters, however, knew that the peasants had for them no greater love than for their lord. They had bullied and punished and betrayed them, and many a serf owed them a debt of vengeance, so they had slipped away with the rest of the household, after the fire, and were keeping close to their lord's heels for safety.

Jockin wished to avoid the village and come upon the track rather higher than the spot where he had met the dwarf, but Barbara would not be satisfied until she had seen for herself the ruins of her home; in fact, Jockin saw it was the only way to make her believe that everything was indeed destroyed and that there was nothing to be gained by seeking in the ruins.

"I do not wish to see it—indeed I cannot bear it!" said Francis, so they left him sitting under a tree with the monkey for company and promised to rejoin him.

Jockin led the donkey by a twisting path and came at last in view of the ruined manor house, its tragic shell such a contrast to the beauty of the early morning that Barbara cried out in horror and indignation.

"How could they? How could they?" she said repeatedly, and spoke no word as the jester led the donkey back into the deeper woods, but angry tears were running down her face.

Her cousin saw them when they came up with him again.

"Was it so very terrible?" he asked curiously. "Indeed, if my father's castle were burned down, I think I would weep too. But there, no one would dare to use him so badly."

"My father thought like that, and see what is left to him!" Barbara retorted. "Who knows that your father, too, has not been ousted by his serfs! Oh, my poor mother!" she wept. "She will take this more ill than she took the loss of Philip. Everything gone! Her terraced garden! Her roses and tapestries! Everything!"

"You did not leave the baby in the village," Francis observed, seeing the child peacefully asleep in Barbara's arms.

She glanced down at it and held it a little closer.

" 'T were a pity to disturb it now," she said carelessly. "The washerwoman is one of our household. We shall come up with her when we join the company."

The road was stony and Jockin could see few signs of Sir Richard's party. He guessed they had not many horses between them. The rest no doubt were still ranging the woods with smoke in their nostrils, maddened by the fire.

Nor dared he travel openly on the road. He had to skirt it, walking beside it among the trees, where there were no signs and no footprints. He trusted the dwarf to leave a sign at the first crossroads.

Meanwhile, though the donkey's pace was slow, young Francis lagged farther and farther behind.

Once he stopped to pick some wild raspberries, and

once to lace his shoe, but he never hurried to make up the pace he had lost, and Barbara shouted angrily at him, hushed by the jester, who feared her voice in the quiet woods.

When they looked at him he limped, and at last it seemed the only thing to put him on the donkey while Barbara walked of her own free will.

"What a history! The page rides while his lady travels on foot!" mocked the jester, to shame the boy.

But the Lady Barbara cried, "So long as it is a donkey he rides, it suits the page better than the mistress!"

Tossing her head, she plucked a handful of wild raspberries and shared them with the child, which Jockin now carried on his arm, and with Philip's monkey, who was chattering with hunger.

"Methinks the crossroads are near," the jester said in a little while, and they crept closer to the road.

A few hundred yards farther on, the road did divide into several ways, each winding carelessly in a new direction through the trees, but so like one another that without a sign Jockin would have been puzzled indeed to choose between them. Leaving the children hidden with the donkey, the jester crept forward to see if anyone stirred at the meeting of the roads. He half hoped to find the dwarf waiting there; then he might have taken the pony for his lady.

But the dwarf was not there, and the four roads were narrow and shaded, arched by the trees.

Where was the sign?

Jockin searched till Barbara grew tired of waiting and came to join him.

"Keep your eyes about you!" he warned her, as they searched different paths.

"I believe horses have passed this way. Here are horse-hairs caught in the brambles!" Barbara said, indicating the path that led east.

"They have been there many days," said Jockin. "The woods are all well used and often. But where is the sign? I told the dwarf to leave a sign."

Barbara still insisted that she had discovered the right path. Farther down she found a piece of silk that she swore had been torn from the litter, and farther yet lay a worn horseshoe that might or might not have lain there many days.

"Say I am right, good Jockin! This must be the path!" she said impatiently. "We have missed the dwarf's sign. He is too stupid to make it clear for us. Come, let us hasten after them!"

Jockin made yet one more search down the western path, which he had not fully explored, and as he came to the bend he found the dwarf's sign at last, a yellow silk scarf tied to a twig.

"It is the dwarf's scarf, I know it well," the jester said, and Barbara agreed with him.

"Then why do you hesitate?" she said. "Let us fetch Francis and the baby and the donkey and be on our way. Too much time has been spent in searching, and my father awaits us."

But Jockin was staring at the ground.

"I see no marks of horses, nor of footprints," he said, shaking his head. "Without the sign I had not guessed a large company had passed this way so recently. That I would not say of the eastern path. I like your first path the better, my lady."

"Nay, those marks were ages old, you said so your-self!" objected Barbara. "And since the dwarf's scarf was put to guide us, what further proof wish you? Only let us make haste that they leave us not too long a drag behind them."

Jockin still hesitated, but Barbara was completely convinced, and nothing would persuade her of any other way but the westward path, so westward they continued, in the shelter of the trees, getting hungrier and more footsore every hour, but hoping each moment to catch up with the main company, who, when they received the dwarf's message, would surely be waiting for them.

Chapter 16

The Wrong Road

At midday they came to a little stream and quenched their thirst.

Jockin marveled to see that Barbara herself made a cup from her hand for the baby, whose hunger had been somewhat appeased by the lump of sweet stuff which was now almost gone. She also washed the sticky remains from its face and hands and surveyed it quite kindly as it sat on the grass.

Jockin, his eyes all about him as before, caught sight of a flat rock upon which were spread some broken scraps of meat and bread. He ran to them eagerly and gathered them up.

"Some have left offerings here for a poor afflicted person, or for a holy hermit!" he exclaimed, holding out the bread with excited hands. "I had never thought to rob a holy hermit, but today I think our need is greater than his, God rest his soul."

The food was not appetizing. Barbara turned it over in her hands and at last said, "Give me the egg that remains. It is clean inside the shell!" But finally she dipped the stale bread in the eggshell and shared it with the hungry baby. Francis was so exceedingly hungry that he ate the scraps without complaining, while Jockin finished what they did not want and craved for more.

He would not let them stay, though Barbara wished to paddle and Francis to sleep in the grass.

"If people bring food here, there must be houses not so

very far away," Jockin objected. "We must not walk on or near the paths lest we be seen."

"It is a strange history, to avoid the *peasants*," grumbled Barbara, "and my father must have traveled fast to lead us yet. I would we might come up with him quickly!"

Her dress was torn by the thick undergrowth, and her shoes were spoiled. Jockin put her again on the donkey, insisting that Francis should hold its head on the farther side so he could not lag behind.

The food, poor as it was, had heartened them and they walked the better for it, but Lady Barbara had privately decided that if her palfrey was not with the party ahead of them, she intended to ride in the litter with her mother. A donkey's back was quite the most uncomfortable seat on which she had ever traveled, and she would have given it up willingly to her cousin had he not been such a miserable crybaby, and deserved to take his turn at walking.

And walk they did. As the afternoon went by, Jockin insisted that they travel faster rather than slower. The little donkey was strong and made no objection, but Barbara and Francis complained bitterly, yet dared not stay, for Jockin's eyes were worried, and he no longer spoke and encouraged them.

He could not understand why Sir Richard had not waited for them, unless the dwarf on his small pony had been longer in coming up with him than any man would expect. And if the dwarf had met with an accident, they would certainly have heard or seen something of him, since they were never more than two stone throws from the path, and Jockin examined it at regular intervals to see whether there came bends and turnings, so they might not lose their way.

He could only think that they must be traveling very much slower than he thought or hoped, and that Sir

Richard's party, pressing forward on account of danger, or perhaps of the indisposition of Lady Isabel, was hastening toward shelter and food for their large company.

Yet why had no one turned back to meet them and bring them up with their lord?

He turned over the matter of the dwarf's scarf, which was so clear a sign he could not believe he had mistaken it. The road remained rocky and he saw no tracks, but he was not able to search as he would have wished, for the sake of faster traveling and for fear of being seen.

And when the woods thinned, he was forced to plunge even deeper into the forest and to avoid the few charcoal huts and other human habitations that sprang up, till he lost the path and lost valuable time finding the way.

It was the page Francis who found it at last, which so encouraged him that for twenty minutes or more he walked most courageously.

"See, the woods are ending, and the road winds on," said Jockin. "When we reach the last fringe of trees, we can perhaps see many miles across the open country, and there, where the road crosses the hills, we shall assuredly see our own company ahead. Only tread carefully that we may see before we are seen ourselves."

The children believed his words, as indeed Jockin belived them himself. They were eager to come out of the woods and, rising rather steeply, mounted a little hillock between the last beeches, and came at last within sight of open country.

Surrounded as the manor house was by thick woods and forests, they were used to the captivity of trees, but nevertheless the sudden sight of rolling downs and hills was like a release from prison.

Jockin felt suddenly exposed and afraid, but the children spread wide their arms and sniffed the cool breezes that came rolling across the valley. The monkey shivered, and clung to Jockin's neck. Nobody was about.

The road dipped between downs to cross a river at a natural ford. There they saw it mount the opposite hill and go winding away westward, now rising, now falling, now hidden between folds of distant hills, now traveling stoutly on the summits, till it merged into evening mists far away in the distance.

The road was empty, all ten miles of it, so far as their eyes could see.

"Watch the folds in the hills!" Jockin counseled them. "That is where a company may be hid a long while before they climb into sight again."

But though they watched every fold till their eyes ached and smarted, no company rose from them, and small golden feathers floated warningly into the sky, the first heralds of sunset.

Worried as Jockin was, the utter calmness and serenity of the open country appealed to him. Here were no ravaging hordes of peasants, banded together for plunder or rebellion. The wide, deserted valleys and hills breathed safety and freedom. He felt as if the woods behind him held danger and the hills were a refuge.

Even if they met an odd peasant or two in this open country, they could hardly harm them. Jockin felt almost sure now that they had taken the wrong road, for all the dwarf's sign. The scarf might even have spelled a warning. A further search down one of the other paths might have revealed a far more certain token, but to return all those weary miles with evening falling was quite impossible.

Somehow they must find some shelter for the night, and, if possible, some food and milk for the baby. In the morning they would make new plans, and surely Sir Richard would send messengers to find them when they did not arrive.

At the bottom of the hill below the wood, Jockin thought he saw the roof of a small hut.

Walking a few paces farther proved that he was right. Moreover, the hut stood on the crossing of two roads, the first, on which they were traveling, running east and west between the forest and the hills, and the other, running south and north, winding its way beside the river for many and many a mile, as empty and deserted as the other.

Barbara was willing enough to ask for food and shelter at this, the only inhabited dwelling within sight, and Francis too followed Jockin with some eagerness as he led the donkey down the hill and knocked at the door.

It was opened by an old woman, who blinked at them in surprise. Behind her shoulder a tall, plain youth stared with his mouth open at the travelers. One felt that, living on the road as they did, they were not unaccustomed to strangers, but the strangely assorted little group with the monkey and their weary donkey quite astonished them. The baby at once began to wail, and Barbara rocked it in her arms.

"Can you give us food, and shelter for the night, good mistress?" Jockin asked.

"Do not call her good mistress! She is but a dirty old woman!" Barbara muttered, when the woman half closed the door and began to discuss the matter with her son.

"Indeed, she may prove our good mistress, and more, if she does not turn us from her door this night. 'Twill soon be dark," Jockin said, "and where else we may find food, I know not. We shall not catch up with my lord tonight. We might even pass him on the road if we ventured farther in the darkness."

"True!" Barbara nodded. Then, growing impatient, she called, "Have you some bread and some milk, good wife, for this poor baby? It starves and cries and has not eaten since noon."

The old woman came out of the door to stare again at the untidy girl with the torn dress and haughty voice. She looked, too, at the ragged tunic worn by Francis, bearing his uncle's coat of arms, sadly torn and stained by raspberry juice. And the jester, the tall, thin youth wrapped in a dark cloak, leading the donkey by a leather thong. They must be of some noble house, but who they were she could not tell, nor what they did in such a sorry plight.

"Tell me first, good mother, have you seen a company of noble people ride this way today?" Jockin asked, as the woman still stared, joined by her son, who gaped as if he had never seen a young lady riding on a donkey before.

"Aye, there was a company this morning!" piped up the boy, and Barbara leaned forward eagerly to hear what he could tell.

"Who were of the company?" she demanded, but the boy seemed frightened by her arrogance; he opened and shut his mouth several times and could utter not another word.

"Did you see the company he speaks of?" Barbara asked the mother.

She shook her head. "Nay, I was in the woods with the pigs. My son tills the land down by the river. He said it was a large and noble company."

"Were there so many? How many were mounted and how many on foot?" demanded Barbara.

The son seemed to have lost all speech, and at the same time Jockin's eyes warned her not to betray them by asking too many questions or describing who or what they were.

The baby now set up another wail, and the old woman's eyes fell on it with some compassion.

"Is that your child?" she asked Barbara.

"Nay!" said Barbara, laughing. "It belongs to—we discovered it in the forest. Can you give us milk and bread for it?"

"The house is small," the woman objected. "Two leagues farther on the road there is an inn."

"We cannot travel farther tonight," Jockin said firmly, "and the child suffers for lack of food. Pray let us come in."

Suddenly the woman relented and opened the door wide. At the same time she signaled to the boy to take the donkey around to the back of the hut, where there was some kind of shed. She flung a wooden bowl after him and told him to fill it with milk.

The hut was so poor and dirty that Jockin's home, in contrast, seemed like a palace. A central fire smoked wretchedly, so that the children's eyes smarted and watered. A kind of platform built at the side of the mud floor served as bedroom; there were a couple of wooden stools, a pitcher, and little else.

"I cannot sleep here!" whispered Barbara in horror. Francis began to snivel and wipe his eyes. The woman stared at them with hostile misgiving.

"The place is poor. I have no room for guests. You had better go to the inn," she said.

Jockin felt that although the woman knew nothing of the peasant uprisings and the burning of the manor house, her poverty and degradation made her suspicious toward them. The wave of discontent sweeping the countryside was to break out nearly thirty years later in open and organized rebellion, but meanwhile the resentment was there, and sparks burned in odd corners, one of which had fired Sir Richard's manor.

When the boy came in with a bowl of milk that was either sheep's or goat's milk, the woman grudgingly offered them some coarse flat bread, nearly baked on the hot stones; it was the most palatable thing they had yet seen in that hovel. The baby eagerly ate pieces of bread soaked in the milk, and Barbara shared what was left of the milk with Francis, both grimacing at the flavor but too famished to reject it.

This time it was Barbara who tended the baby, and having fed it, she took the dwarf's cloak from Jockin, wrapped the child in it, and laid it to rest on the primitive bed in the corner.

The woman's eyes opened wider to see Jockin's quaint clothes.

"Art thou a fool?" she asked curiously.

"Aye, a very fool to have brought these young ones to such straits!" agreed the jester, sighing.

"Whence do you come?" she insisted.

"From the land of fools!" sighed the jester, turning over in his mind how best to put her off. Fortunately at that moment the boy interrupted him by crying out, "I saw a fool in that company this morning!"

"Nay, that were not possible!" said Barbara. "A dwarf maybe, but no fool."

"I saw a fool," the boy repeated, nodding, "with a cap and bells, and one red stocking and one yellow, and he carried the head of another fool on a long wand, with long ribbons that flew in the wind. He rode up and down beside the company on a piebald horse, plaguing them right lustily, and the ladies threw him sweetmeats."

"Did the ladies not ride in a litter?" Jockin asked.

"Nay, they all rode their palfreys, tall, like men, and very merry," answered the boy, glib enough now to describe what he had seen. "I saw no litter, and no dwarf among them."

"Did they come by the way we came?"

"Nay, but from the river road, close by where I was toiling," he said. "I saw them coming a long way off."

"And did they take the road across the hills?"

"Nay, they traveled south, on the way to Bristol."

"Did they bear a coat of arms such as this?" Barbara cried, indicating Francis' travel-worn doublet.

"I saw none," was the reply.

"It was a *strange* company!" cried Barbara, shedding tears of bitter disappointment. "We shall not overtake my father after all!"

Soon after, she flung herself down on the mattress of heather beside the sleeping baby, and Francis crept into another corner beside the wall.

Daylight was fading rapidly, and the fire gave no light. The two peasants laid themselves down more or less where they were, to sleep till daylight returned, while Jockin propped himself up on a stool, with the monkey on his lap, to watch his sleeping charges and make plans for the future.

Chapter 17

The Journey

Jockin must have fallen asleep, for he awoke in the cold morning to find Barbara shaking him by the shoulder.

"We must be on our way! I cannot stay here any longer!" she cried passionately.

At the same time the donkey began to bray in the shed and the peasants awoke. The boy went out to fill the bowl with milk, while the children and the monkey helped themselves to what remained of the flat bread, watched by the woman.

"Have you money?" Jockin asked Barbara, who sometimes carried a small purse at her belt. She nodded, and handed a coin to the woman, who seemed satisfied, but her curiosity was great, and she constantly plied Jockin with questions as to their circumstances and their business in traveling so strangely together.

To stop her inquisitiveness, Jockin asked questions in his turn. Was that part of the country peaceful and contented? To whom did the land belong? Was she a freewoman and her son a freeman? And what towns lay farther along the road across the hills?

She replied that the country was peaceful enough, but times were hard since the Black Death, and no one was particularly contented. She herself had lost her husband and all her neighbors of the sickness. The land belonged to Sir Hugh de Lacey, and she and her son were his serfs. She tended his lord's pigs while her son tilled his land and fished in the river. Their wages were poor and they both worked hard for long hours. Things would never be better—the poor woman sighed—so one had to put up with them.

Sometimes a passerby made them a little present in return for milk or bread, but it was not often. Their house was poor, as Jockin could see for himself, and never likely to be better.

"Let us go!" said the children impatiently.

The road ran westward, to Wales, the woman told them, and the lower road by the river turned back into the woods.

"That is the road we will take!" said Barbara, when the woman was out of hearing, but Jockin objected.

"Nay, there is danger in the woods," he said, "we should not go back to meet it, but go boldly onward. It comes to me that my lord will surely go to take shelter with his brother in Wales, then we may be there as soon as he."

"To my father's castle!" cried Francis in delight. "Oh, why did you not think of that before? But my home is miles and miles away from my uncle's house!" he added, becoming despondent. "Well mounted as we were, it took us nearly a week of riding. How can we travel there on foot, and with a baby, and with one small, miserable donkey between us?"

"Why, we can journey *anywhere!*" cried Barbara in great contentment. "If my father is there, as I feel assured he will be. Good Jockin, let us go immediately."

They left the hut as the woman was already setting out for the woods with her swine.

Barbara mounted the donkey with the baby on her lap, but she was soon pleased to give her place to Francis; her perch was so uncomfortable, and the morning so bright and golden, that nothing pleased her better than to run beside the road on the dewy grass, picking bright flowers to put in the baby's hands and listening to the larks that caroled above their heads in the brilliant sunshine.

Poor Jockin! To him Wales was a single point in his destination. He did not know the border of that far, wild country stretched wider than ten times the length of the great forest he had left.

He led his weary little company mile upon mile southwestward and out of their way, when by good fortune at a crossroads a wayfarer put them on the road to Shrewsbury and they began to walk northward, knowing that through that city Lord Simon had ridden from his castle in the north of Wales, now many months ago.

Time after time the tired children would demand if Jockin thought they might come to Shrewsbury that evening, or the next, or the next—Barbara doubtfully, since she better remembered the long ride there in the spring, Francis peevishly, as if asking drew the town nearer.

Jockin put them off with what encouragement he could find to comfort them. The great world was so new and strange to him. It would be a miracle if ever they did reach Wales, but feeling their dependence on him, he promised that all would be well and, to keep their spirits up, asked every passerby if a company of people had passed by, with a litter among them, and a dwarf riding on a black pony.

No one had seen such a company, and though travelers were few and far between, Jockin could not believe Sir Richard had come that way. But neither was there any sign of a peasant uprising, and no more burned houses. It was as if they had left a bad dream behind them, but they knew well enough there was no returning.

Barbara had a little money in her purse. They were able to buy food all that day and the next, and to pay for better lodging for the night.

Barbara grew more and more attached to the baby, doing everything for it herself, and becoming jealous if Jockin carried it, or if Francis made it smile. The baby became the center of their cavalcade, the point of interest upon which they could all agree. They admired its curly hair and sunny smile and agreed that no baby was ever so courageous or intelligent, and that it had grown and developed considerably in their company the few days they had been upon the road.

As the weather continued warm and fine and every hour brought them a little nearer his home, Francis lost his fretful ways, put up with his footsoreness and poor food, and stepped out like a man.

He also discovered a fund of long and entertaining stories, mostly told him by old Eustace, his father's fool, and these passed the weary miles pleasantly, entertaining his cousin, and giving Francis sufficient importance to keep him well content and bold of heart.

On the third night they arrived at a tavern that Jockin distrusted from the moment they came to the door. But the children were exhausted, dusk was falling, and Jockin had no mind to be out wandering on the roads with them at night.

The landlord was surly and his guests were few. He brought them a meal of sorts, but as they sat eating it he approached the table and demanded to see their money.

Jockin knew the purse was nearly empty, and trembled when Barbara turned it inside out, to discover only a few small coins that he knew would not cover the cost of their lodging.

The landlord angrily protested that it would not even pay for what they had eaten.

"Then I will give you a jewel out of my cap in the morning," said Barbara carelessly.

The landlord's greedy eyes flew at once to the cap that Barbara wore inside out by Jockin's advice.

"Show me the jewels!" He demanded.

Barbara pulled the cap from her disheveled hair and displayed the gems Sir Richard had brought his daughter from abroad. They glittered splendidly in the rushlight, and the host winked at them covetously. He said no more, however, but left them to their supper.

"You should not have shown him your jewels till the morning," Jockin said, but Barbara yawned widely, and soon afterward went to bed.

Lying on the hard floor outside the guest chamber, Jockin fell at once into a deep sleep. The anxiety and fatigue of his daily traveling did not allow him to watch. He needed all his strength to encourage the children and bring them all safely through the day.

He awoke suddenly in the dark, with the feeling that something had touched him, or had passed by him so closely that it resembled a touch.

He lay wide awake, listening.

Then suddenly steps passed him again, silent and swift. Something leaped across his prostrate body at the same time that Lady Barbara inside the room began to cry out, "He has taken my cap! He has taken my cap!" while the monkey chattered angrily beside her.

Jockin leaped up, and ran, not into the guest room but down the stairs. In the kitchen by the light of the dying fire he perceived the landlord, who, approaching him with every appearance of concern, cried out, "What is amiss? Why does my lady cry out so?"

But Jockin saw he was in his bare feet, and thought he held something concealed behind him.

The jester was perplexed. Already the other guests were waking and stumbling heavy-eyed into the kitchen. It was not simple thing to accuse or attack a landlord. If he was innocent, all the guests would be on his side and Jockin would get a drubbing for his pains.

But he watched the man's movements carefully, for fear he might conceal what he was holding about his person, or in some corner of the room.

The landlord was breathing fast, as if he had been running, but he received the jester with civility.

"What do you want, Sir Fool? Is your lady dreaming? Can I serve her with mead or bread?"

"Nay, she cried out on waking," replied Jockin. "She is in a strange place and did find herself for the moment affrighted."

"Then how can I help you good Jester?" said the man. "What do you want in my kitchen at this hour?"

"I could not sleep either, and my bones froze within me," said Jockin. "I wished to warm myself at the embers before I slept again."

Two or three of the guests joined him in huddling around the fire. The landlord kicked the embers into a blaze and sat down among them. Jockin noticed that he still kept his left hand behind his back and guessed that he knew he was being watched.

"Do you know," Jockin began to his neighbor, "which hand a man more readily puts out for money?"

"The right!" said one. But another cried, "The left!" and a lively argument began.

"Nay, how can a man tell through argument?" said Jockin. "Thinking too deeply makes false servants of a man's actions. But I will prove it to you." He drew out of his pocket a few precious coins Barbara had entrusted to him for payment in the morning.

"I will toss these in the air," he said, "and we shall see by which hand a man seeks to enrich himself!"

As he spoke, he tossed the small coins in the air. The guests snatched at them laughing, some with the right hand and some with the left, but the greedy landlord grabbed with both, letting drop behind him Barbara's little silken cap, which Jockin immediately picked up and held tightly.

The whole company saw him do it. They saw the sparkling of the gems in the jester's hand, and looked from them to the landlord's face. They recognized the little silk cap as belonging to the ragged noble girl whom the jester escorted.

Nobody spoke. Jockin turned and left them, carrying the cap in his hand, but he had the feeling that had he asked them to do so, the guests would have drubbed the host out of his own house.

"Jockin! Jockin!" called Barbara's voice from the guest chamber. "Where have you been? I have called you till I am hoarse!"

"I have your cap!" Jockin answered in the doorway. "Sleep fast and say no more."

She obeyed him, but the jester watched all night with his back propped against the door.

In the morning they left without further payment, and the landlord pretended not to see them go.

"I think men should not know you carry jewels," Jockin said, when the inn was a mile behind them.

"Then I will take them off my cap and you shall carry them," said Barbara, snatching the cap off her head and pulling away at the gems. "One, two, three, four, five! Shall we be in Wales five days from now, Jockin? Or what shall we do to pay for food and lodging?"

Jockin was worried by the same thought. Nor did he think it was safe to pay with jewels, so far beyond the value of the hospitality they received. At any time they might be stolen, and in any case his loyalty to his master made him unwilling to part with the gems.

But they must eat, and later in the day they would have to offer one for bread.

Meanwhile, they had eaten before leaving the inn, and the morning was fine and sunny.

Every hill brought the cry from Francis, "There are the mountains of Wales!" and the snubbing rejoinder from his cousin, "Those hillocks and bumps! Then why have you so boasted of your mighty mountains, Cousin Francis? I see nothing of any importance—nothing that any man could call a mountain!"

"We have first to pass through Shrewsbury," Jockin reminded them both to stop their wrangling.

Hunger came as the morning advanced, for they were young and had walked far.

"We must eat!" Barbara cried from the donkey's back, shifting the peevish baby from side to side. "The child is starving, and I am as hollow as a cask!"

"I too!" complained Francis, who had fallen behind, as was his wont when things went badly with him.

"Buy food for a week with one of my jewels!" Barbara said, and this Jockin agreed to do.

They came to a village, and while Barbara and the baby sat down on the grass to graze the donkey, Jockin went away to look for food, taking Francis with him to carry what provisions they could find.

The baby seemed to thrive on their strange journeying. Though hungry at present, it was rosy and fat. But Philip's little monkey was moping and sad. Accustomed to pampering and lavish attentions, he now had to be content with what scraps the others did not need, and to sleep on hard boards instead of a silken cushion.

It hated to be parted from Jockin, and whimpered when he was out of sight.

Between scolding the poor monkey and preventing the

baby from attempting to pull itself up by the donkey's hind leg, Barbara was fully occupied till a sudden chattering from the monkey made her look up.

A man with a bear was walking down the road toward the village.

The bear was ragged-coated and mangy. The man led it on a chain, but it seemed too spiritless to do anything but follow him.

Barbara had seen such a bear before, brought into her father's hall and put through tricks that amused the household well enough, but nothing to the show Jockin had made with his animals.

She felt sorry for this wretched beast, but the baby and the monkey began to cry with fright.

The man grinned and stopped in front of them, whereupon the monkey sprang onto Barbara's shoulder and clasped its arms around her neck.

The donkey, also frightened of the bear, laid back its ears and trotted some distance off, while Barbara was left, half throttled by the monkey, clasping the bawling baby.

"Be off on thy business!" she told the bear master. "Do not dawdle here frightening children and chasing away my donkey. Be off to the village, where doubtless you will get a welcome for your draggled beast!" The man laughed at her rudeness, but eyed her keenly.

"You are not of some traveling company yourself, then?" he asked, looking at her once fine gown, the monkey, and the white donkey now grazing tranquilly once more by the roadside.

"Aye, we are traveling to Shrewsbury," Barbara replied with her usual candor. "How far may that be, can you tell me?"

The man shrugged his shoulders. "Days, weeks even,

with such a caravan," he said, glancing at the baby. "Do your animals perform for money?"

"Nay!" said Barbara contemptuously. Then she added, "But our jester has taught them a handful of tricks more amusing, I vow, than any played by that skinbag your bear!"

At that moment Jockin and young Francis approached across the village green.

When he saw his lady in conversation with a stranger (and such a stranger!) Jockin began to run, fearing she might say too much, or be rudely answered, and when he saw the jester approaching, the man's grin faded and he stared with great curiosity at him and the page.

"And do you, too, travel to Shrewsbury?" he asked.

"Aye, we do," Jockin answered curtly, sending Francis to catch the wandering donkey. "Do you know that town?"

"I know it. I am but newly come from there," the man replied.

"Did you meet a company in the town, or on the way thither?" Barbara cried eagerly. "A great household with servants and horses, a litter, and a dwarf on a black pony? Did you not meet them on the road?"

"I met them not," was the reply.

More and more bitterly Jockin blamed himself for not returning after the first night to take the other road at the crossroads. What the dwarf's sign meant he did not know, but that it had led them terribly astray he saw more clearly every day.

"Thy lady tells me her animals perform right prettily," the bear master said. "Do you show them on the road?"

"Nay," Jockin said, but in that moment the idea was born, and when the bear and his master had passed out of sight, he spoke of it to Barbara and Francis.

"Even the jewels will not last for long," he told them.

"People hesitate to take them, and when they do, they give no true value for them. When they are gone, we shall have nothing left to sell and must starve."

It was quite true. Barbara looked down at the remains of her once beautiful dress, at her tarnished girdle and ragged shoes. There was nothing that would raise a penny among them except the donkey, and how would they carry the baby or manage without him? Barbara felt herself getting more tired and footsore every day, although she was too proud to complain as Francis often did. But now she looked at Jockin with a great fear in her eyes.

"What shall we do? Will we die on the road?" she asked.

"Nay, yonder bear and his master have put a plan into my head," said Jockin. "We will see if Sir Philip's little monkey and our donkey yonder remember the tricks I taught them last winter. Then, if a bear can earn his master's living, why, we should not starve either."

"What! Act like common people! Show off the animals' tricks for money!" cried Francis in horror. "It is impossible! We could not!"

His obvious dismay checked the disgust on Barbara's face.

"Of course we could not! We are not clever enough!" she said tartly. "But Jockin could; the animals will do anything he tells them and people will flock to see them."

"Oh, well, if Jockin does it! We need not be near," said Francis, mollified.

But in spite of Jockin's confidence and Barbara's hopes, the plan was not so easy as they had expected.

The donkey had plodded many dusty miles since it left the manor house. It was no longer the playful pet and occasional steed, but a beast of burden, working from sunrise to sunset. It had no inclination to play tricks or show any life whatever.

And Philip's little monkey likewise, torn from rich food and comfortable housing, had grown thin and sulky, spiteful with everyone but Jockin, jealous of the donkey and of the baby.

"It is of no use!" Barbara sighed, when they had lost nearly a whole morning trying to persuade the two animals to do their tricks. "We shall never, never do it. But we still have my jewels. Perhaps they will last us till we get to Shrewsbury and then we can borrow money from my aunt, the Lady Abbess, to get us to Wales."

Shrewsbury! It lay like the land of promise ahead of them, like the turning point of their fortunes. For in Shrewsbury lay shelter and surely welcome, if the sickness had left the convent, and here above all they were bound to hear news of Lord Richard and his household, since they must have passed through the town to get to Wales. And surely he would have left some token, some message for them to explain why he had not waited or returned, and why the dwarf had marked the wrong road.

"You should beat the animals!" Francis said angrily, while Barbara only sighed hopelessly.

But in the end Jockin's patience was rewarded. With much kindness and unending tolerance, he persuaded the donkey and the monkey to perform two or three simple tricks, which, with some somersaults and tumbles of his own, made quite a little show.

Barbara was determined not to witness it when the time came to attract a crowd on the next village green, so she took the baby aside and settled herself under a large chestnut tree at some distance from the jester and his animals.

Francis had unwillingly to hold the donkey, and it was only the knowledge that all except the last jewel had been spent that kept him to a task he thought to be so undignified. He stood as aloof as possible behind his charge, but all their hearts were beating fast. They watched every house and every passerby for the expected audience.

It was a very small village, but first a few children, then a peddler, two or three women, and an odd man or two arrived. These swelled to nearly twenty people, old and young.

They stood between Barbara and the performers, so she could not see if the monkey was sulking or the donkey being stubborn. She could not bear to sit there in ignorance, so she picked up the baby and crept to the outskirts of the crowd.

There she noticed for the first time how ragged was the donkey's coat, and the monkey, who had been scratching incessantly of late, surely had a patch of mange. Her cousin looked pale and tired. She knew they were all unkempt and dirty, all except the baby, which she washed and tended in every stream they passed—but was that shabby travel-stained fellow walking on his hands really the jester of Sir Richard of the manor house? She felt ashamed of him, but whatever her own feelings, the crowd was well pleased. The people clapped and shouted, and in sudden shame at herself, Barbara, too, shouted, "Bravo, Jockin!" and brought the eyes of the crowd upon her.

Blushing and humiliated she walked away, and was joined a little later by the jester and Francis. Jockin showed her a few small coins in his hand.

"They were all so poor," he exclaimed, "we could not expect much from them."

"It will not pay for a meal, nor even for half a meal!" complained Francis, and Jockin had insisted on rewarding the animals with some of the small stock of bread remaining to them.

"If we praise them and feed them, they will act better for us," he said.

"How can animals understand? It was different at home, where there was plenty of everything," said Barbara, "but here where there is so little, and worse to come, we should have saved it for the baby."

Jockin said nothing, but he gave his share of the dinner to the baby, who had a prodigious appetite.

That night they could not pay to sleep at a hostel, which they reached when the animals were too tired to perform.

"Now if you were a real and proper jester, like old Eustace, you could amuse the company with lively tales and play tricks upon them, and they would give you money for us all," said Francis petulantly.

"Do not despise Jockin!" cried Barbara, her eyes flashing fire. "Who else could have saved us from the fire or brought us safely all this way! Shame on you, Cousin!"

Francis looked ashamed and said no more.

"There is the jewel left!" Barbara said. "Let us pay for the lodging with that."

But Jockin was firm.

"We must keep it. Who knows the day may not come when we need it more sorely than tonight," he said. "The air is warm—we must seek shelter elsewhere."

"I do not want to sleep out of doors again," said Barbara, remembering the dew-soaked awakening in the forest.

"I will find shelter," said Jockin, and despite their complaints he led them out of the village and on till they found a ruined hut.

The slopes close by were thick with bracken, turning golden brown in the late summer's sun.

This Jockin plucked in the gathering dusk, till his hands

were torn and bleeding, but three thick and springy beds were spread on the floor of the hut.

Here they slept well all the night long.

In the morning they returned to the village, when the animals were rested and fresh, and gave a performance outside the hostel.

The guests of the previous night were preparing to leave, packing their horses and chatting with the host.

They gathered around Jockin and applauded the efforts of his animals, who did their tricks well enough, being rested, and the donkey, at least, well fed from a feed of green grass outside the hut.

This time the coins flung were heavier, and they left the village knowing that tonight they could pay for a good supper and a proper bed.

Their hearts were lighter; everything seemed more hopeful and promising. The travelers had come only one day's hard ride from Shrewsbury—surely they might reach it in two?

The road ran across hills. Now they were high and now low. Each time they climbed, they hoped to see the town they longed for in the distance. Barbara looked for the silver glint of the river and Francis for the hills of Wales. As they reached each summit, they tried to race each other to see what the view might bring, and always it was just another hill. Till Francis, growing discouraged, lagged behind again, and Barbara, running ahead, uttered such a cry that even the donkey pricked its ears, and Jockin hastened to see what had caused her such excitement.

Almost incoherent in her agitation, Barbara was pointing down the next valley.

"Look! There behind those trees! They disappear! They are coming out again! I can see them! I can see them! I can see the litter and my father's white horse, and oh, surely that is Melisande—yes! And all our household! They are coming to meet us!"

At her elbow Jockin peered, his heart thundering against his ribs. Was it possible that Sir Richard's party, having failed to find them on the other road, had come to seek them on this? Or had the dwarf in truth not come upon them till lately, and explained the sign and the mistake he had made in marking the wrong road?

But the greater Barbara's excitement and the longer they both looked, the lower sank Jockin's heart. By the time Francis joined them, the jester felt fully convinced that this time it was Barbara who was wrong. The company they were looking upon, for all they had much the same appearance as Sir Richard's household, was another company, and again they were doomed to disappointment.

Francis, who was longsighted, agreed with him.

"That is not my uncle!" he said bluntly. "See, they are all mounted, while we know that half our horses ran away."

"They took horses in Shrewsbury!" cried Barbara, refusing to be dissuaded. "See, I can almost see my father's beard!"

"The rider on the white horse has no beard!" said Francis. "And when would my uncle's squires wear green doublets?"

"They are scarlet! I can see they are scarlet!" passionately repeated Barbara.

"They are green!" Francis said scornfully.

Jockin said nothing. The tears that ran down Barbara's cheeks were streaming in his own heart.

The company began to mount the hill, and now not even Barbara could pretend she knew the coat of arms or recognized the riders. She bowed her head on the donkey's neck and sobbed bitterly in her great disappointment.

Francis tried to comfort her.

"Do not cry, Cousin. We are soon in Shrewsbury now," he said kindly. "There we are sure to hear news and maybe we shall even see them."

Jockin did not wish to lose an opportunity of filling their purse. He led the animals aside onto a greensward and began to put them through their tricks.

Never had he played with a heavier heart, while the donkey and the monkey seemed dull and spiritless, though obedient to his voice.

Barbara turned aside, too wretched to care, so that Francis had to hold the baby, and the donkey, too, when Jockin required it.

As the jester had expected, the company stopped at the top of the hill, to rest and enjoy the spectacle. They were a crowd of noble gentlemen and ladies. Their fine clothes and glittering harness reminded Barbara of all she had lost, and she wept more bitterly than ever.

One of the ladies seemed about to speak to her, but the girl gave her a look of such fierce pride and scorn that she turned her head aside abashed. Only when they had gone did Barbara remember she had asked no news of her father.

"Did you inquire of them?" she asked Jockin eagerly.

"Nay, I forgot," he replied, weighing their now heavy purse, and unwilling to tell her that no one in that cavalcade had heard a word of Sir Richard and his company.

Francis opened his mouth to speak, but a look from the jester silenced him.

Presently, to console her, he said, "The lady in the litter was not half so handsome as my lady Aunt Isabel."

Barbara gave him a brief and wintry smile of gratitude.

Chapter 18

The Potion

Barbara's spirits did not rise all day, and although at nightfall they found reasonable shelter and good food at a small wayside hostel she would not rouse herself to eat, and Jockin began to fear she was ill.

Indeed, before the evening was out she was in a high fever and delirious, calling out for her father and her mother, and not knowing Francis or even the baby. Jockin alone seemed to soothe her. He stood by her bedside holding her fevered hand, at his wit's end with anxiety and terror.

Once more he blamed himself, this time for not using the jewel the night before. Who knows what sickness might have been lurking on the damp floor of the ruined hut? Maybe even the Black Death itself had been waiting there.

But the host's wife, a kind and motherly soul, set his mind at rest on that point at least. She had known and nursed the Death too long not to recognize it, she said. This was another fever, the outcome perhaps of long days and nights of exposure, for Francis and Jockin had between them told their whole story to the sympathetic woman, who, shocked and curious, put Barbara in her own bed and nursed her like a child. Francis had perforce to act as nursemaid to the baby, keeper to the monkey, and groom to the donkey, while Jockin was occupied in soothing his sick charge.

He took his duties sullenly, but performed them well enough, and was somewhat placated when the baby, with the fickleness of the very young, turned to him as readily as it had turned to Barbara and soon quite bewitched him with its favors.

The long night wore on. The host's wife slept, snoring, for some of the hours, but Jockin did not sleep, while Barbara tossed and turned. How it recalled to him his first night in the manor house, with his lady like this, hot with fever and damp with chills, calling his name aloud and clinging to his hand.

She had recovered then, but perhaps she would never recover now. In those days she had been well fed, well clothed, and lay in rich apartments. Now she was ragged and had been often hungry, eating coarse food, and lying in the hard bed of an innkeeper's wife.

And in the morning she was worse, lying so still that Jockin held his own breath to watch her breathe. How he longed for her mother, or for Father Francis to recite the prayers that he could not remember. Awed by fear, Francis recited a Latin prayer. Jockin murmured his own words in his own language, but he did not expect God would answer the prayers of a poor jester.

The host's wife looked very grave.

"She should have a potion," she said. "In some sicknesses the sweats kill, but in others they cure, and this is one of those. We should get her a potion from the wise woman."

"Where can it be procured?" Jockin asked eagerly.

"Half a day eastward from here," the woman replied. "You could reach her soon after noon on your donkey. The wise woman asks good money for her potions. Can you pay?"

Thankfully Jockin felt his well-filled purse. Yes, he

could pay, even though the host's bill might be a heavy one and they might be forced to stay there several days.

He waited only to receive directions for finding the wise woman, and then rode away on the little white donkey, leaving Francis in charge, and the kind hostess watching over Barbara.

Day after day the patient donkey had plodded on, usually with a burden on his back. He had submitted to performing tricks for Jockin and had supped on poor grass or rich, just as it came.

Now he was mounted by Jockin, who, being the heaviest, had walked before and moveover was forced into a gallop that lasted over hill and dale. His flanks were kicked by Jockin's heels, his sides were belabored by Jockin's fist, he was not spared where the ground was rough, but urged across streams, pulled through undergrowth, and rested for only a brief time every hour.

The sturdy little beast did his best, and so it was that soon after noon Jockin came to the filthy hovel described by the wife of the host as the wise woman's home. Bunches of herbs hung from twigs around her cottage. Her simples betrayed her calling.

With a great sense of relief Jockin swung himself over the back of the sweating donkey and called her name.

He knew these women—half recluse, half outcast—who lived their strange, wild lives far from the homes of their neighbors, following their odd calling from interest and for the sake of the money it brought them. Some of them were immensely rich, he had heard, as rich as they were clever, and as clever as they were rich.

But this one had nothing to show of her wealth as she tottered to the door of her home with her hair hanging down over her eyes, and such rags upon her body that it was a wonder they held together.

Yet to his astonishment Jockin found that he knew her, since she was neither more nor less than the crone who had approached them on the riverbank on that other journey to Shrewsbury. So long ago, it seemed, when they had traveled and returned on the other road, the road they should have been traveling today.

She recognized him at the same instant, and a gleam came into her beady black eyes.

"Good day, Sir Jester!" she croaked. "Do you ride again to Shrewsbury?"

"Aye, I ride to Shrewsbury, good dame," Jockin replied, and suddenly the whole meaning and result of their previous encounter struck him with such force and clarity that he could only stare at her transfixed.

"And your lady, is she in her convent?" the wise woman asked, with the gleam of malice that spoke so plainly of her great knowledge.

"You know she is not," Jockin replied.

"And that fine house she spoke of. Does it yet stand?" asked the crone.

"You know it does not," said Jockin.

"And you, Friend Jester, has it all befallen you as I told you it would?" pursued the crone.

"Suffer greatly I have, and am still suffering," replied the jester soberly. "And render service have I done also, in rescuing Sir Richard's daughter. But cause them suffering I have not done, since they know not she is ill, and have word that she did not die in the fire as they supposed. I have come for one of thy potions, good mother, for my lady lies sick of deadly chills and fever. When she is recovered we will on to Shrewsbury, where we hope to meet with Sir Richard, or have news of him. Hast seen aught of him, good mother, in thy wanderings?"

"Nay, I have not left my house this many a day," muttered the wise woman. "The damp of the river puts pains into my bones. But you are sure of my potions, Sir Jester, if you speak so certainly of your lady's recovery from such an illness"

"The host's wife did say she had only need to sweat," said Jockin, looking frightened, "and she did say your simples made most powerful potions. I will pay well for it, good mother, if you will give me a sweating potion to cure my lady."

"You will need to pay!" the wise woman replied, as she hobbled back into her hovel.

She was gone a long time, and glad as he was to rest and to graze the donkey, Jockin was in an agony of impatience when at last she appeared. She carried a little bag in her hand.

"Steep these in stream water and give them to your lady," she said. "By midnight she will sweat, and the fever should be gone by morning."

Jockin thanked her, trembling with joy, and asked the price. The sum the wise woman asked was so excessive that he was struck dumb and did not know what to do. It would take every penny in his purse to pay for the potion, and there would be nothing left to pay the host and the kind hostess for their hospitality and lodging.

The donkey would be too tired to perform next day; moreover, they would be unlikely to come across such a rich company who would pay them so handsomely again. But he dared not refuse the wise woman and began slowly to count up the coins in the purse that belonged to Barbara.

"You will need the money to pay your host," said the wise woman cunningly. "I will take the jewel you carry inside your doublet. Innkeepers do not like to be paid with jewels; questions are asked and things become unpleasant. But no one will ask such questions of the old wise woman."

Again Jockin was paralyzed by her knowledge. For a moment he hesitated, and then slowly put his hand inside his doublet and drew out the jewel he had placed there for safekeeping. The Lady Barbara's last jewel. But it was to save her life.

"Poor boy," the wise woman said pityingly, as her hand closed greedily over the prize. "The worst is yet to come for thee. Thy charges will be off thy hands these three days hence, safe among their kind, but thou wilt not find thy couch of velvet so quickly!"

"If my Lady Barbara and young Sir Francis find their parents so soon, then indeed my couch is made of gold itself!" Jockin exclaimed joyfully, but the old crone only shook her head with an enigmatic smile.

With the precious little bag clasped in his hand, Jockin mounted his donkey and set out for the inn.

His head set for home, the donkey traveled bravely, and despite the wise woman's words Jockin's heart was light. In three days his charges would be safe, she had said. What more could a poor jester ask? If Sir Richard, having no house, had no more use for him, or could not afford to keep him, if he had to walk every step of the long way back to his parents' house, Jockin did not care—his charge would be fulfilled. Therefore, his thoughts were happy ones.

Chapter 19

In Shrewsbury

Jockin found the Lady Barbara much the same as when he had left her. The host's kind wife was still watching beside her, while Francis, anxious and miserable, had allowed the monkey to bite the baby, and was impatient for Jockin's return.

The child was not injured, but it had cried a good deal and the host had complained.

When Jockin set foot on the stairs, the little monkey rushed to meet him with a chatter of pleasure, and the baby called out joyously. Jockin entered the sick chamber with one on either arm and the precious bag of simples in his hand.

Barbara lay barely conscious, not able to recognize him, but it was Jockin and not the host's wife who at last persuaded her to open her lips and swallow the bitter draft he had prepared.

Some time later she fell into a quiet sleep. By midnight she awoke in her right senses and her brow was damp. She slept again, and by morning the fever had left her.

She was weak and exhausted; it was not possible for her to travel that day, but by evening she could stand on her feet and walk, leaning on Jockin's arm.

After a second night's rest she said she was fit to travel and would wait no longer.

Jockin put her on the donkey's back. They paid their bill and said farewell to their host and his kind wife, who filled a bag with meat that would last them till they came to Shrewsbury.

Now our journey is nearly done, thought Jockin, stepping out thankfully on the last lap of the road. Certainly we are intended to come safely to the end of this strange adventure.

But nightfall found them still some miles from the town. With Barbara still so weak, they were forced to rest long and often. Francis grumbled at carrying the heavy child, but Barbara was too feeble to support it safely. Jockin took it on his arm, which made the monkey jealous, and everyone was discontented.

They spent the last night in a traveler's resthouse of mean aspect and poor food, but the meat in their bag consoled them. They had not enough money left to pay for better lodgings had they found them.

By noon the next day they came to Shrewsbury.

When he trod the cobbled streets again, Jockin marveled to think of all that had happened since his previous journey. Had he really ridden through these same streets on a fine gelding, in gay motley with an embroidered saddle cloth and a silk cushion strapped behind him for the dwarf to ride upon?

Where was the dwarf now? Was he dead? Or had he really betrayed them? Jockin, who loved his fellowmen, hesitated to think so badly of him.

He could not remember the road to the convent, and was forced to ask it. His clothes were now so torn and travel-stained, nobody recognized them for the uniform of a jester.

Although Barbara, in her excitement sat upright like a noble lady on her donkey, she was as ragged and dirty as any common girl. Her hair hung wild and unkempt about her shoulders. She had nothing to comb it with but her fingers. They had all torn strips from their clothes to bind their shoes, which were falling to pieces, and people wasted few glances on such ragged travelers. A few smiled at the laughing, rosy baby, wondering to which of the three gaunt young strangers it belonged.

Francis trod lightly now. He felt he was on the threshold of his home, and henceforward would know every step of the way. He looked to left and right for the sight of a familiar face, a glimpse of his uncle's coat of arms, or even his father's. He forgot his ragged clothes and matted hair, walking like a prince. He amused himself afresh with the baby, taking it from Jockin and letting it try its little legs and feet on the firm cobbles. To their delight it was beginning to walk, and took its first steps in Shrewsbury streets.

At last they entered the narrow street to the convent, and here Jockin's thumping heart beat in suspense and agony. Would the doors still be closed? Would they still be barred out by the sickness? Would any of the nuns remain? They knew so little of any other life but their own gypsy wanderings.

The street seemed ten leagues long, and every pace familiar, but at the end the doors were open, and the gatekeeper, an aged sister with a hundred wrinkles on her face, bid them come in, with a look of surprise.

She who saw many travelers wondered at this strangely assorted party, of which the girl spoke like a noble lady, and looked like the poorest in the land.

She wondered still more to hear this strange girl demand to see the Abbess.

"Our Lady Abbess is at her devotions. It is Mother Angeline who has care of travelers."

"The Lady Abbess is my aunt," said Barbara in a faint voice. She stumbled from the donkey to a bench in the corner of the entrance hall and sat down, half fainting.

Later, supported by two nuns, she was led alone into the presence of the Abbess, who received her with compassion and kindness. She had not met her niece before, but did not doubt her claim, even if her likeness to Sir Richard had not called her his child.

"But what do you here alone?" she asked, in dignified curiosity.

"I am not alone. I have my cousin Francis with me, and Jockin, my father's jester, who saved us."

Though revived a little by food and wine, Barbara was almost too tired and exhausted to answer questions.

"Saved thee from what?"

"From the fire. My father's house was burned to the ground. Did he not tell of it?"

"I have not seen thy father."

"Not seen my father?"

Now Barbara sat erect, her startled eyes anxiously fixed on the calm, wimpled dignity of the face before her. "But did he not visit the convent in passing?"

"He has not passed through Shrewsbury since the day in spring when the sickness in the convent turned him back," answered the Abbess. "You were with him then. I thought he had brought you now. It is true, my child, that he has not traveled with you?"

"No, no!" sobbed Barbara, with the tears streaming down her face. "We sought him here. We were so certain he had passed this way on his journey to my uncle in Wales."

"He has not gone to Wales," said the Abbess, "else he had passed through Shrewsbury, and he has not been seen in the town since that day in spring. I expected him to bring you shortly, now that God has taken our sickness from us. Tell me of that fire you spoke of, my child, and of this journey. . . ."

Barbara poured forth the story, while at the same time Jockin was telling it to a group of eager sisters in the refectory below. Like Barbara, he had his hopes dashed when he found no trace of Sir Richard, and he spent the whole of the long night wondering what next to do.

But the problem was solved for him by the Lady Abbess. She had immediately taken her brother's child under her protection. Not only was Barbara in poor health but it was out of the question for her to venture a step farther from the safety of the convent walls. Sooner or later, news of Sir Richard would arrive, and the convent was the most suitable place to await it. The baby, too, had been adopted by the delighted nuns, and even if its mother never claimed it again, the convent would care for it and bring it up.

As for Francis, a party of merchants was leaving Shrewsbury in the evening for Wales. The Abbess made it her business to know what went on in the town, and she had moreover ascertained that they would let the boy ride with them to his father's castle. The Lady Abbess would provide him with a horse, for the convent owned great property in the country around.

Barbara, aware now of her great weariness and of the rigors and exertions of the long, desperate journey they had made, was relieved at the thought of staying a while in the quiet, busy convent, tended by kind hands and with no more question as to where to spend the night or how to get their food. She was glad not to be parted from the baby, and proud to show many of the ignorant nuns how an infant should be cared for.

She parted affectionately with her cousin Francis, who was fretting with impatience to reach his home. Their joint adventure had brought them closer, and Barbara had to admit that Francis had become more of a man than the sickly page they had brought with them from the manor house. She wished to send the monkey to her brother Philip, but the little creature had never loved Francis, and clung so piteously to Jockin that Barbara had not the heart to part them.

"Tell my brother that his monkey is safe and well," she said.

They parted. Jockin saw young Francis mounted in his new cavalcade, made his good-byes, and watched the boy's pale, happy face turn once more to salute him before he rode off to Wales.

Three of his charges were now accounted for.

There remained only the little monkey and Jockin himself.

What should they do? The convent fed them. Jockin had a good rush bed on the kitchen floor, and the nuns were wonderfully kind to him, greatly entertained by his account of the fire and their adventures on the road.

But the next morning Barbara called him.

"Dear Jockin, I wish you to go home. I cannot wait. I must have news of my father! Get you back toward our house and ask news of him at every mile. Then, when you do obtain it, send word to me as quickly as it can fly."

The Lady Abbess also urged him to travel homeward, gathering what news he could from all sources. She wished to know how far the rebellion had spread and if others had suffered like her brother. She thought of her own peasants and the vast lands owned by the convent. Discontent was catching, and all houses burned alike. She, too, urged Jockin to send word at the earliest opportunity. She offered him a horse, which the jester gladly accepted, accepting also the purse of gold that she gave him for his needs on the road.

Then he knelt and kissed the hand of the Lady Barbara, who, with tears streaming down her cheeks, implored him to return to her the moment he had found her father.

"For without you I should not be here," she said, "and in your absence I am like to lose myself again."

But Jockin had no fears for her safety in the hands of her aunt the Abbess within the convent walls.

Chapter 20

Betrayed

Jockin left Shrewsbury with a light heart, and the knowledge that he had fulfilled his task. Eagerly he looked forward to the meeting with his lord, and later witnessing the reunion with his daughter.

Swiftly passed the miles beneath his horse's feet, while landmark after landmark brought back memories of the first journey to and from Shrewsbury, for now he took the road by the Severn, and he well remembered every bend.

He asked questions of every wayfarer and at every tavern, but Sir Richard was not known. It was not until he had again entered the great forest that he heard word of him, and by then his horse was lame and he was forced to take him to a smith.

When he asked his usual question, the smith replied, "Aye, when his house was burned down, Sir Richard went straight to his friend the Earl of Dean, who has his castle not twenty miles away from the manor. From there he does conduct his business and see to the building of his new house."

"And the rebellion? Do the peasants yet revolt?" asked Jockin anxiously.

"Nay, I think not. I have heard some were punished, while the rest toil to rebuild the house. Sir Richard was ever a strict lord, but I have heard tell he is much stricken and quieted, having lost his eldest daughter in the fire."

Jockin started at this news. So he had not received the message! Then some ill must have befallen the wretched dwarf, and thus it was no one had searched for them.

"More than a broken shoe is here amiss," the smith said, tapping the horse's hoof. "The frog itself is damaged. He will not travel for a day and a night, or more."

"Then I must leave him with you!" exclaimed Jockin, impatient to be off. "He belongs to the Lady Abbess of the Benedictine Abbey at Shrewsbury. See ye do guard him well till she sends for him."

The smith was not unwilling to hold such a handsome horse as security, and when Jockin had paid him he took to the road on foot, turning over these new tidings in his mind and wondering what to make of them.

He wondered again, as he had wondered a hundred times, what part his father had played in the rebellion and what had been his punishment if he had been caught.

As he trod again the familiar paths of the great forest, his parents and his home became nearer, dearer, and more desired. He longed to go straight to the humble hut and find his mother, to tell her the long story, and to hear what news she had to tell him.

But his first duty was to his lord, and he resolutely took the straightest road toward the castle of the Earl of Dean. The little monkey, who had traveled all this way on Jockin's shoulders, became more lively in the woods, as if he recognized them again. Jockin found hazel nuts for him, and a few late, overripe raspberries. Missing the children, the baby, and even the companionship of the horse, he was glad to have the company of this helpless little animal. By resting very little and walking all night, Jockin came to the Castle of Dean in the evening of the second day after he had left the horse with the smith.

The great castle looked formidable, and the water was

dark in the moat that ran around its walls. The drawbridge was double guarded as if for siege, Jockin thought,
for Sir Richard's tragedy had made his neighbors uneasy,
and the houses of the nobles were carefully protected night
and day.

When Jockin told his name to the first man-at-arms,
several pairs of eyes stared at him with curiosity and
suspicion.

"Sir Richard's jester!" bawled the man-at-arms across
the drawbridge. A second man-at-arms conducted Jockin
across a second drawbridge, where he was handed over to
a new man-at-arms, who led him across the central courtyard into the main hall.

Overwhelmed by the grandeur of this great castle,
Jockin walked with trembling knees and downcast eyes,
afraid to look for what he longed to see, a glimpse of his
lord's livery or coat of arms. The monkey clung shivering
to his neck, hiding its face in Jockin's long hair.

But in the crowded hall he was recognized.

There was no need for the squire to call, "Sir Richard's
jester!" before half a dozen pages and squires, with the
old, dear coat of arms embroidered on their breasts and
sleeves, came tumbling to welcome him and clap him on
the back.

Their welcome was so exuberant that Jockin could not
find his tongue, but stood panting with grateful tears in
his eyes, waiting for them to release him.

And while he waited and the squires still shouted at and
buffeted him, steps strode down the hall, parting the
curious groups that had gathered.

Sir Richard, summoned by his special page, arrived
with white face and searching scrutiny to meet his jester.

At his heels trotted the dwarf, alive and well.

Jockin had only a few words to say.

"My lord! Your daughter is safe!" was the message he

had prepared, the message that he sought for now on coming face to face with his lord. But the sudden sight of the dwarf, as healthy, apparently, as ever, and with a malicious smile on his lips, unnerved him, even as the realization of that dreadful betrayal came upon him with an overwhelming shock.

His eyes dropping from Sir Richard's face to the dwarf's, they met each other in a long, blank stare, which was broken by Sir Richard's voice.

"Where have you been?" he asked, in low, bitter severity.

Still stunned, Jockin could not answer yet.

"I sent you to find my daughter," Sir Richard continued in the same low, threatening tones. "What account have you of her?"

"He let her die, and himself escaped!" suddenly broke in the dwarf with a spiteful croak.

Jockin started. "Nay! That was not the message I gave you in the forest!" he exclaimed.

"I met him in the forest, as I told my lord," the dwarf croaked. "He told me the Lady Barbara and young Sir Francis had perished in the fire—the fire that was started by his father! He had time to save only his own skin and the monkey. He was always crazy about the beast!"

"Nay, it is not true! Lady Barbara and Sir Francis are safe and well!" cried Jockin, shocked by the dwarf's flagrant enmity.

"Where are they?" demanded Sir Richard.

"My Lady Barbara is at Shrewsbury with her aunt, the Abbess," replied Jockin, trembling. "And Sir Francis is ridden to Wales, to his father's castle."

"At Shrewsbury! How came my daughter there?" exclaimed Sir Richard.

"We walked, my lord, with the white donkey," said Jockin.

"They walked to Shrewsbury! My lady walked every step of the way!" mimicked the dwarf, laughing mockingly. "My lady in her silken slippers, she *walked* to Shrewsbury, riding for pleasure on the back of the white donkey! And the young puling page ..."

"Be quiet!" shouted Sir Richard. "Do not insult my dead daughter, nor my nephew, my brother's child. Tell me your story, lad."

Trembling in every limb, poor Jockin could scarcely find words to begin. Had he been closeted alone with his lord, he felt the tale might have flowed forth to convince him, but with the malevolent dwarf waiting to contradict or betray him at every opportunity, and the household crowding around to hear every word he might utter, he was almost out of his senses with confusion and despair.

"We took to the woods," he began haltingly. "In the morning I returned to the manor. It was a smoking ruin. I met the dwarf yonder on a black pony. I told him my lady was alive."

"Nay!" sneered the dwarf. "He told me she was dead!"

"Indeed, I begged the dwarf to tell my lord the Lady Barbara was alive!" pleaded Jockin. "And I did pray him to leave a sign on the crossroads in the forest that I might follow when we came after."

"I left such a sign!" said the dwarf.

"Aye, but not on the road you took!" cried Jockin.

"The road to the east!" said the dwarf.

"The sign lay on the road to the west!" said Jockin.

"Nay! I did lay it on the eastward path," insisted the dwarf.

"And I did find it on the westward!" said Jockin.

"Nay! You found it on the eastward and so avoided it!" said the dwarf triumphantly.

"What was the sign?" asked Sir Richard.

"A silken scarf tied to a twig," said the jester.

"He knows it!" cried the dwarf. "You see, my lord, he saw it, and came not, being afraid."

"And from whence are you come?" Sir Richard asked him sternly.

"From Shrewsbury town, my lord Richard."

"From Shrewsbury town also!" cackled the dwarf. "Not content with walking there, he walketh back also! And how many days did it take you, friend fool, to walk this great journey?"

"I walked not back. The Lady Abbess did lend me a horse," said Jockin.

"And where is the horse?"

"He went lame at the edge of the forest, and I left him with the smith," confessed poor Jockin.

"He did leave the Lady Abbess's valuable horse with a strange smith!" mocked the dwarf. "Why did you not lead him beside you, poor fool?"

Jockin could not reply, for he had never thought of it.

"Why not?" repeated Sir Richard sternly.

"I did make haste to come to your lordship," he said lamely, "I did not wish to wait on account of the horse."

"And why did you go to *Shrewsbury?*" demanded his lord.

Again poor Jockin stumbled and sought his words. "At first . . . methought my lord was ridden that way. Then . . . methought not. But . . . I was afraid to return. . . ."

"Aye, indeed he was afraid!" sneered the dwarf. "His father fired the house! He himself let the Lady Barbara die. He did well to be afraid."

"Nay—I thought my lord might be—at Shrewsbury, or heard of there!" pleaded Jockin. "Methought after the fire he had ridden to Wales, to his brother Lord Simon, for shelter. . . ."

"What, with all my company! And my Lady Isabel half

dead with fear and grief?" said Sir Richard scornfully. "Only a fool would run so far from his home; wise men seek to cure their disasters. I have a good friend here in the Earl of Dean, and thanks to his help my new house already stands a man's height from the ground."

"His tale is false!" piped the dwarf. "Why should he think you to be in Wales—or in Shrewsbury?"

Sir Richard scowled terribly and, addressing the jester once more, charged him. "I ask thee—what became of my daughter?"

"She is in Shrewsbury, my lord."

"And my nephew? Fear not. I charge thee not with his safety, only with hers."

"He is in Wales, so I believe, my lord, at his father's castle."

"It cannot be true!" said Sir Richard. "It is not possible they have walked so far."

"It is a lie!" added the dwarf. "This man has been hiding in the woods—look at his clothes, his hair, and his broken shoes! See how thin he is! He has been hiding from your displeasure, and now, being hungry, and thinking his deeds forgotten, he has come back to thy service."

"Did my daughter send a sign, a token, by thee?" Sir Richard demanded, ignoring the dwarf.

"None, my lord," said the unhappy Jockin.

"Nor my nephew—nothing?"

"Nothing, my lord."

"Why not?"

"Because she—he—I had not thought of it. . . ." Jockin trembled.

"Because she is dead, and young Francis too!" screamed the dwarf.

Jockin was stunned; he could find no words to justify himself, no truth that the dwarf could not twist into a lie.

He was put in the charge of two men-at-arms who

were not of Sir Richard's company, and from them learned that directly after the fire a servant had been dispatched on horseback to Wales, to break the news of his apparent death to Francis's father, Lord Simon, and of the death of his sister to Philip.

This servant, being originally of Lord Simon's household, had remained, neither had he tarried in Shrewsbury on the way, or told his news, but ridden with all speed to take the news to Wales.

Sir Richard had intended to ride himself to visit his sister the Abbess, and thence to his brother's house, but the Lady Isabel had been so desperately ill following the loss of her daughter in the fire that he had not been able to leave her. She was only now slowly recovering, and Sir Richard was determined above all to keep the news of the jester's return from her. She must not be agitated by these wild and unlikely statements. He warned the household, and said Jockin must be kept out of the children's sight.

In the evening Jockin was brought to the great table where sat Sir Richard with his host and friend the Earl of Dean, the dwarf in close attendance.

For an hour they questioned him until in his terror and bewilderment he scarcely knew what he replied. Everything he said was contradicted or twisted by the dwarf. They laughed him to scorn when he spoke of the washerwoman's baby. Yes, a small child had been lost in the fire, but not even a fool would carry a baby into the woods, much less to Shrewsbury.

It was so evident from the beginning that neither his own lord nor the Earl believed him that Jockin became completely disheartened and hardly roused himself to answer their questions. He heard the dwarf spin a net of lies that he had not the strength to contradict, and his weariness was such that he scarcely listened.

He longed to pour out his tale to Father Francis, but the priest was at his lady's side, offering her what comfort she could find in these dark days.

It was almost with a sense of peace that he found himself at last taken down two flights of damp, green stone stairs beneath the castle and flung into a dungeon below the moat, so dark, damp, and cold that it might have been the moat itself.

All night Sir Richard tossed and turned, much disturbed by the jester's unlikely story. Though he did not, could not, believe it, the mere doubt that had arisen about his daughter's fate was enough to trouble him greatly.

The Earl saw the anxiety in his ravaged face, and offered in the morning to send a man in haste to Shrewsbury, that his mind might be set at rest.

All day long Sir Richard could not make up his mind to accept his friend's offer, as if he could not bear to have his last shred of hope taken from him, but at nightfall he agreed to the Earl's proposal. Only, he said, he would go himself to see his sister, the Abbess, and ride on to offer condolences to his brother in Wales.

But a new difficulty arose. Maids or pages had tattled, and the Lady Isabel had become aware of the new rumor in the castle. She insisted that a rider be sent immediately to find out the truth of it, but was equally determined that the messenger should not be her husband. In her anxiety and nervous agitation she could not bear have him leave her side.

"Send Edmund!" she repeated, naming the groom, "and bid him return hotfoot. For this uncertainty will be my death."

At that moment the dwarf offered himself as messenger.

"Let me go, my lady," he proposed. "The Abbess knows me well. If there is aught to tell, she will relate it fully to me. I will not rest till I am there and back again."

"What better messenger than our faithful dwarf!" cried the Lady Isabel joyously. "But what of your poor bones, good Dobbin? You who so dislike to ride! You shall be faithfully rewarded, and I will send a page with you to carry your comforts."

"Nay, I can ride alone!" said the dwarf hastily, but his lady insisted, so in the end he was obliged to set forth on one of Sir Richard's best horses, with a young page on another at his side, and they left the castle riding fast into the forest.

Sir Richard and his lady found it was hard to conceal their impatience until his return. Sir Richard took no further interest in the plans for his new house, his wife could find no comfort in her younger children. She wept and cried over them and spent the day wringing her hands in a transport of anxiety. Father Francis could neither calm nor comfort her.

And then on the following evening, horses' hooves clattered across the drawbridges, and a cry arose in the courtyard.

"The dwarf is back! The dwarf is back!"

Sir Richard came hurrying into the hall as the dwarf staggered in, dusty and sweating. Lady Isabel, white-faced, came in from her apartments and, supported on her husband's arm, cried to the traveler to tell his news, if news he had to tell.

"Sad news indeed, my lady," the dwarf said in a low voice. "Before we had left the forest, we came upon a smith who had received news by travelers of Shrewsbury town. It appears that the Death did ravage the convent to such intent last spring that all but a handful of the nuns are dead, and the Abbess retired to live upon the convent estates in the country."

"Then the jester lied!" said Sir Richard with deep emotion.

Lady Isabel swooned away, and in the confusion no one questioned the page who had ridden with the dwarf. But he talked to his companions, as boys do.

"Nay, I heard nothing. The dwarf would not have me near him, and each time he made inquiry, he left me to hold the horses. But when he did receive the news ye heard tell of from the smith at the edge of the forest, the smith's boy came to take my horse for me, and seeing a fine gray horse close by the smith's hut, I did ask the boy to whom it belonged. Whereupon he told me, 'To the Abbess of Shrewsbury.'"

Meanwhile, the lady had recovered and retired with her women to her chamber, and the Earl of Dean and Sir Richard had rounded on the dwarf and were rating him soundly for returning so early instead of pressing on to find out whether such a rumor was true.

"And if it is true," Sir Richard said, "then you had done better to ride on to Wales to ask advice of my brother, rather than return before you had well set forth on your journey."

While they were railing him, Sir Richard's page, a boy of quick intelligence and much boldness, came forth to tell his masters what he had learned from the other page, and the boy was at once brought before them.

"Is it true that you did see a gray horse at the smith's, belonging to the Lady Abbess?" Sir Richard demanded.

"Aye, my lord, I saw it," said the boy.

"There was no horse!" screamed the dwarf.

"Who told you to whom it belonged?" the Earl asked the page.

"The smith's boy told me himself," replied the page.

"He was but boasting to you. The horse belonged to the smith," cried the angry dwarf.

"And did the dwarf tell you the message he had from the smith?" demanded the Earl of Dean.

"Nay, my lord earl. But before we came to the smith's place, he told me we need go no farther than this, and when he had parleyed with the smith, he did tell me that our journey was ended, and in any case he had not intended to ride farther when he started."

"It is not true!" shrieked the dwarf.

"Quiet!" roared Sir Richard. "Tell me, boy, did the smith say aught else that you heard?"

"As we turned our horses' heads for home, the smith cried out, 'Why go ye no farther? I had some keys wrought for the convent door I had hoped ye would take to the Abbess.' "

"This tallies not with your tale!" the Earl said, angrily turning to the dwarf. "Why, I say, did you return so soon? I charge you that your tale is false, conjured to save yourself a long journey. Your servant lies to you!" he said to Sir Richard. "Who knows but that all his tales are false! He who serves you ill on a small errand is like to serve you worse on a great one. Have him imprisoned till his falseness is proved!"

Sir Richard had no further interest in the dwarf's fate. This time nothing could prevent him from riding himself to find out the truth of all the conflicting rumors. Summoning the young page to accompany him, and without even bidding farewell to his wife, he had fresh horses saddled and rode out into the moonlit night at breakneck speed.

The Earl, who had no compassion or mercy for the dwarf, threw him at once into the dungeon to await Sir Richard's return.

Chapter 21

The Prisoners

Thus it was that Jockin received in his prison the most unwelcome companion that fate could have provided for him.

He had already a companion of a kind, for the monkey still clung to his neck when he was taken down the dungeon steps, and the sufferings of the poor creature in the damp and the darkness occupied him fully for the first few hours of his imprisonment.

In the morning, when a plate of unappetizing scraps and a pitcher of water were brought him, a little pale-green daylight glimmered through the barred window that peered out, he guessed, just above the surface of the moat. It was too heavily barred for him to see anything with certainty, but it seemed to look across the water to a dark-green wall that supported the drawbridge.

The monkey was terrified of spiders, of rats, and of toads. The dungeon abounded with all these creeping things, and in comforting the poor little beast, Jockin lost some of his own horror and despair.

He now blamed himself a hundredfold for not defying the dwarf and beseeching his lord to send a messenger immediately to Shrewsbury to prove his story, and that Sir Richard had actually done so he did not know even on the third evening when, to his utter astonishment and dismay, the dwarf was pushed into his dungeon by the jailer and the key turned upon them both.

Jockin had counted himself lucky not to be fettered

by the leg irons that he saw attached by iron stakes to the floor, but when he met the dwarf's fierce and malevolent gaze, he began to wish that, after all, each of them had been chained to his own corner.

The monkey, however, quelled the dwarf's vengeful air. He shrieked and chattered with such savage intensity that Jockin was forced to hold him firmly, or he would have sprung out of his arms to attack the little man in no uncertain manner.

The dwarf eyed him with fear, removing himself to the farthest possible corner of the dungeon, where he lurked in sullen silence.

Caged in a dungeon with his known enemy, Jockin awaited the night with a kind of dread. He knew the dwarf had done his best to destroy him. What revenge might his twisted mind contrive to put into action under the cover of darkness? Nothing was too evil to believe of him now.

As the daylight disappeared, so that each was only a shadow in his own corner, Jockin pressed the little monkey against his chest for comfort, and their hearts beat together in fear of the long darkness and the horror of their fate.

Jockin could not sleep. Long after the monkey had fallen asleep in his arms he sat upright on the cold, damp floor, listening for some movement in the dwarf's corner. But what he heard surprised him and stirred his compassionate heart.

For the dwarf was groaning.

A victim to rheumatism and the pains of old age, he was accustomed to a warm dry bed of rushes, protected by curtains and tapestries from drafts and damp.

Here on the dungeon floor, with mists from the moat mingling with condensation from the wet earth under the stones, he trembled and shook and was seized by such fearful cramps that he could not contain his moans.

Jockin's pity overcame his dislike. Putting the monkey down carefully, he crawled toward his unfortunate companion and began to rub his tormented limbs.

At first the dwarf resisted with angry gasps between his groans, but the strong and soothing power of Jockin's hands overcame his anger; he relaxed his poor crooked legs to the jester's ministrations, his groans subsided into sighs, and he lay quiet.

"My corner is not so damp. Let me help you thither," said Jockin, putting his strong arm around the dwarf's shoulders. The dwarf resisted at first, then complied.

Jockin scraped together what he could find of the dirty straw that covered the floor and settled the dwarf upon it. The indignant monkey he ousted from the corner and held in his lap. Once more the cramps assailed the dwarf's limbs, and once more Jockin rubbed and massaged them into peace. Then, huddling together for warmth, the three strange companions slept until morning.

When the gray-green light returned and the jester awoke, he found the dwarf's eyes fixed upon him with a look of wonder, almost of admiration, so different from his usual malevolent expression that it quite transformed his ugly face, giving him an expression that was almost beautiful.

After staring at him a long while, the dwarf suddenly crept back to his own corner and sat there without a word.

When the jailer brought their food, they shared the broken meats together, and Jockin noticed how the dwarf held back, instead of grabbing, that the jester might serve himself first. Only when Jockin fed the monkey did the dwarf begin to angrily protest, but he checked himself before he had uttered two words, and was silent.

The long day passed and the night was spent exactly

as before. The dwarf went to sleep in his own corner, awoke groaning, and was rubbed and tended by Jockin till his cramps left him. Then they slept side by side till morning.

Still the dwarf spoke no word, nor would he answer when Jockin spoke to him. Only, when the dim light came back, he often stared at the jester, with that softer, wondering expression that glorified his poor, ugly, twisted face and purged the hate from it.

On the second evening, when the jailer came to bring their evening meal, the dwarf suddenly broke his silence to utter hoarsely, "I wish to speak a word with Sir Richard!"

"Sir Richard is not here!" returned the jailer shortly.

"Bring me to the Earl of Dean," said the dwarf.

The jailer only laughed curtly, and clanged the door of the dungeon, turning the key in the lock. The dwarf sank his head in his hands.

Jockin was about to comfort him with the advice to be patient, since when word came from Shrewsbury, as come one day it must, all would be well—but he remembered that this day must surely spell disaster for the dwarf, whatever crime had thrown him into the dungeon. So he held his tongue, and left the better portions of their unappetizing dinner to his share.

On the third night the dwarf suffered worse than before. His limbs seemed tied in dreadful knots that would not straighten themselves. He cried out till the monkey whimpered in fear.

Jockin would have given all he had for a few of the wise woman's simples, or a thick bed of straw on which his suffering companion might rest. He rubbed and kneaded until at last the pains subsided and the dwarf lay still.

Jockin made him as comfortable as he could and waited

for him to sleep, but to his surprise the dwarf began to talk instead.

After one or two gasps and stutters, as if he could not find the words he sought, the dwarf began, "I served you ill, Jester."

"Aye, you served me ill," Jockin said with a deep sigh. The remembrance was still full of bitterness, and in all his pity for the dwarf's pain, he could not discover why one creature should serve another so badly.

"I have always served you ill," continued the dwarf.

"That is true," Jockin agreed without malice.

"I have always hated you," the dwarf murmured, without emotion, even with some regret.

"I know not why," said Jockin.

"You were always loved," said the dwarf. "Even at the beginning the little children, who scarcely knew you, loved you dearly. Your parents loved you. Even fate loved you, since you recovered from the Black Death, where so many died. Soon the pages and all the household loved you. The animals were possessed by you and did whatever you commanded. And all this when you had been but a few months in the house. Favorite of the Lady Barbara, smiled on by Sir Richard; only Lady Isabel listened to me, the only one in the manor who showed me any kindness. For, after all those years I lived there, nobody loved the poor dwarf. I was ugly and disagreeable, and nobody liked to look at me. I made nobody laugh. When I was a tiny misshapen boy, my parents dropped me at the door of the manor house. When I grew up, I followed my lord, but he never liked me. Lady Isabel pitied me and took me for a grotesque plaything. The children hated me. 'I'll give you to the dwarf!' I heard their nurse say when they were naughty. Can you picture, Jester, what it is like to be so unloved?"

"I would have loved you," Jockin said, "had you not forbidden me, and mistreated me in all the ways you were privy to. Was that sense, friend Dwarf?"

"Nay, it was too late then for love or friendship," said the dwarf in the darkness. "When I was young I craved for it and received none. Even the Lady Isabel has no heart for me. She loved me more to spite the rest, who hated me. When I grew older I lived to be comfortable, and when you came, and threatened my comfort, I hated you."

"Your hate did not serve you well," said Jockin. "Hate is like to turn and smite the man that hateth. What brought you here, friend Dwarf?"

"My lord found out I lied when I set out to ride to Shrewsbury," replied the dwarf simply. "I told my lord I had inquired of the smith at the end of the forest, who told me the convent was shut down and most of the nuns dead; therefore it was not possible for you to have left the Lady Barbara among them. But the page who was with me saw the Lady Abbess's horse in the smith's stable and did tell Sir Richard, which did bear out the tale you brought, and gave me the lie."

"The horse the Abbess lent me!" said Jockin joyfully.

"Aye, that horse. And now Sir Richard himself has ridden to Shrewsbury to find out the truth, while the Earl of Dean, mistrusting me, had me flung into prison. He had better have hanged me directly, for my master will do no less when he returns."

Jockin's eyes shone with joy and relief in the dark dungeon.

"So my lord is ridden to Shrewsbury!" he murmured thankfully.

"Aye, and is likely to return directly or to send word, for no doubt he will find there what he loves most dearly," said the dwarf. "Therefore would I fain confess my guilt to the Earl of Dean that he may hang me directly and so save me from more of these fearsome cramps that do torment my bones. For if I must die, let it be sooner rather than later," he said, shuddering.

"Tell me. The sign—was it on the eastward or the westward path?" Jockin asked curiously.

"On the westward. But we did ride to the east," the dwarf replied. "I did purposely deceive you; neither did I tell my lord of your message, but let him believe his daughter was dead. My shame is deeper than this darkness, Jester, and now the cramps are come upon me again, and I suffer! I suffer! And you will not succor me because I have brought you much grief!"

But Jockin's hands soothed the dwarf's limbs as before, and when the cramps were over, the jester asked, "Tell me one thing more. Was it true my father was there at the burning of the manor house?"

"Alas!" wept the dwarf, worn out with pain and humiliation. "It is true he was there, but he had no part in it. He did come after to seek you, and did break his heart, believing you to have perished. Oh, how I suffer! How I suffer!"

Jockin wept for his parents as he rubbed the dwarf's legs. All these weeks they had thought him dead. Perhaps it was better, for to know he was in prison would have hurt them even more cruelly.

All night long the dwarf suffered acute attacks of cramp and fever. In the morning he was so ill that even the jailer became alarmed.

The dwarf lay moaning, calling alternately for Sir Richard and the Earl of Dean.

"What has he to say?" the jailer asked Jockin, puzzled.

"I know not," replied the jester, reluctant to reply.

The jailer left the dungeon, but the dwarf could not eat the food that he had brought. He drank some water and relapsed groaning on the dirty straw. Jockin sat beside him, pillowing his head upon his lap, while the monkey ate the breakfast the dwarf could not touch.

Meanwhile, the jailer had sought out the Earl of Dean, who was perturbed at hearing that his friend's dwarf lay sick unto death, since Sir Richard had not ordered his imprisonment, and he did not wish him to die before his master's return.

So he ordered the jailer to bring him up into the central hall that the Earl might have a look at him.

But when the jailer went to fetch him, the dwarf clung to Jockin like a child, refusing to go unless the jester accompanied him.

Once more the jailer approached the Earl, who impatiently commanded that the prisoners should appear together.

Jockin almost carried the dwarf up the stone stairs from the dungeon. Once in the great hall of the castle he set him on his feet—supporting him with his arm. The monkey sat blinking on his left shoulder, for even the dim light of the great hall seemed bright after the dungeon and hurt their eyes.

Members of both households, who had heard the story, gathered in little knots to stare at and discuss the prisoners. Some believed one and some the other.

Sir Richard's servants sided to a man with Jockin, but those of the castle thought the dwarf's tale more likely, and asked why the jester had not brought a token from his lady for her father.

The Earl of Dean, seated at one end of a long carved

table on his dais, looked searchingly from one to the other of the prisoners. Then, fixing his eyes suddenly on Jockin he shouted, "Tell me thy story!"

His fear of the Earl almost overcame the poor jester, but with a desperate effort he opened his mouth and began to relate all the adventures that had befallen him since he first woke to find the house in flames.

When he came to the episode of the baby, there was a cry from the listening crowd, and a woman sprang forward to fall on her knees before Jockin and the Earl. Jockin recognized her at once as the washerwoman.

"Is my child living? Is it safe?" she cried, snatching at Jockin's rags.

"It is safe with the sisters at the Benedictine Abbey at Shrewsbury," he told her, and the wretched woman wept for joy.

"And what say you?" the Earl shouted at the dwarf.

"I say the jester's tale is true!" whispered the dwarf.

The Lady Isabel had approached unnoticed and now stood behind the Earl of Dean's chair, with tears streaming down her cheeks. At the dwarf's words she came forward suddenly and, putting both hands on Jockin's shoulders, kissed him on both his dirty cheeks.

For safety's sake the Earl commanded that both men be still kept prisoners and strictly guarded until Sir Richard returned to prove their story true, but while he gave Jockin into the hands of the men-at-arms to keep in the watch room, he ordered the dwarf to be flung back into the dungeon, since not even Sir Richard could care whether he lived or died, so wickedly had he sworn and forsworn his tale of lies.

But Jockin protested loudly, swearing that if the dwarf was sent to the dungeon, he would go too. He could not bear to think of the wretched creature suffering there in the cold and damp with no one to help or comfort him, and when she saw his anxiety, the Lady Isabel joined in his plea that the dwarf might be given a dry bed somewhere in the main part of the castle.

The men-at-arms treated Jockin with rough good humor and curiosity. He was well fed and much questioned. Nevertheless, the days passed slowly till his lord's return.

Once Lady Isabel came to see him. That she believed his tale he could no longer doubt. After listening to his whole story again she thanked him over and over for what he had done for her child, and asked if there was aught he desired that she could do for him.

"One thing only, my lady!" Jockin said humbly, "that one be sent to my parents to bear them news that I am alive and well. And while that one is there, that he may ask my mother for such simples she has as will cure the cramps. For the dwarf suffers greatly, my lady, and he is old and unloved, which is the greatest hurt of all."

Lady Isabel promised it should be done.

Chapter 21

Jockin Is Freed

At last a rider came galloping to the castle.

Jockin dozed in the watchhouse, where the afternoon sun painted a warm patch on the bench in the corner. He dreamed the little white donkey had run away with Lady Barbara upon its back, and he was just springing up to catch it when he awoke, and behold! A horseman came galloping over the drawbridge, through the barbican, and into the courtyard.

Jockin had a glimpse of the horse lashed and foaming with sweat before it clattered out of sight.

The men-at-arms poured out to see, the household assembled, and all the castle folk clustered around the strange rider, who was not Sir Richard, but a man in the service of the Abbess of Shrewsbury.

The first thing he pulled from his wallet and put into her mother's hands was Barbara's little blue cap, shabby and travel-stained, bereft of its jewels, but so familiar that the Lady Isabel uttered a cry of joy.

"Your daughter greets you," the messenger said. "She is well, and in the care of her aunt, the Lady Abbess. She bids me say that the child, too, is safe with the sisters. My lord is ridden on to Wales to see that his nephew is safely arrived, but he will return this three weeks hence. He bids me say: Free the jester and reward him well."

As may be imagined, the Lady Isabel was not loath to do this.

Dressed in fine new clothes, spoiled, and made much of, Jockin felt bewildered and abashed. Favored by his lady and the Earl, worshiped as a hero by the squires, pages, and castle servants, he seldom had a moment to himself. He was happiest with Lady Isabel's younger children, who were delighted to see him again and could not have enough of his company.

No more was said about sending the dwarf back to the dungeon, since Sir Richard had not spoken of his punishment but had only said, "Free the jester."

The Lady Isabel had, in fact, sent for the simples Jockin had asked from his mother, who, rejoicing greatly to hear of his safety, had sent a message imploring him to come to her as soon as he could be spared.

When that joyful day arrived, Jockin set off on one of the Earl of Dean's own horses, his heart as light as air, his saddlebag filled with good things for his parents.

He had bidden farewell to the dwarf, who was better housed than he had been, with warmth and good food. The medicine, it seemed, had cured his cramps.

"Tell your mother," the dwarf said, "that she has a better son than my mother had."

"As for that," Jockin returned, "had your parents loved you as mine loved me, you might have been a better son to them."

He rode into the high morning with great joy and thankfulness at his lot. Every word spoken by the wise woman at the river had come true. Even Bess, the giggling maid who had attended Barbara, was now affianced to Walter, one of the menservants, who had rescued her on the night of the fire.

The peasants had settled to their old routine, he had heard, but he met no known faces on his way home. How familiar and dear were the great woods that had once bred and had since befriended him! And how familiar the tangled paths that he had once tramped and now cantered over so lightly.

He fairly trembled with joy when he leaped at last from the saddle and knocked on the humble door of his home.

His mother opened it, her face a mixture of joy, astonishment, and wonder. "Our son! Our son has come on a horse like a nobleman to visit us! And once we thought him dead!" she said.

Plow Jockin came soon after from his work. He clapped his son on the shoulder and could find no words to speak.

That night they sat long over the embers and talked and questioned as they had never talked before.

One thing more Jockin had to tell them. Lady Isabel had asked him to choose his reward. He had asked to make his father a freeman. When Sir Richard returned, this plea would be put before him, and Jockin had little doubt it would be granted. He had also asked a pardon for the dwarf. He was so old and infirm, what good could be done by hanging or imprisoning him?

And by their very positions in the household, Jockin felt that here was a friend who could become more to him than any of the rest, since the dwarf had renounced his jealousy and now wished only to serve him and to redeem his evil ways. Father Francis had promised to plead for him, and the priest held great sway with Sir Richard.

So when Jockin left them next morning, it was difficult to say whose heart was more full of joy, his father's, his mother's, or his own.

By a whim he rode first to the village to see the ruins of the manor that he had last seen smoking so many long weeks ago.

Now, to his surprise, for he had forgotten what he had heard of it, he saw the foundations of a new house rising. Some of the peasants building it were known to him, and he learned that the ringleaders of the burning had been caught and punished, that one was John-of-the-Field, another the leader of the small company at Lob's hut, and a third Jack, the groom.

As he rode around the walls of the new building, Jockin saw a little group standing at a distance, looking too. They were on horseback and appeared to be three men and a lady. As Jockin stood watching them, the lady, on a gray horse of great beauty, broke from the group and came cantering toward him.

To his great joy he saw it was the Lady Barbara, mounted on the Abbess's horse, her cheeks as pink as ever, her eyes bright, her health as splendid as it had been before their journey.

The other riders hastened after her. Sir Richard and his elder son ahead, and young Philip, well grown and tanned, behind them.

Barbara's delight in seeing Jockin was echoed by her brothers and their father, who was bringing all the children home to cheer and comfort their mother, who had suffered such grief on their account.

Barbara had to know everything that had passed since Jockin had left her, and great was her indignation to learn how the Earl had treated him.

"He had no right to punish our jester!" she protested.

"He did but command in his own house," her father said. "He did it for the best."

"Ugh! That dwarf! I always hated him!" Barbara shuddered. "I hope, my lord, that you will have him sent away."

"My lord, his aging years will quickly dispatch him

farther than you can send him!" Jockin pleaded. "Let him remain. He will do no more harm, my lady. There is no more hate left in him."

"You never hated any man, good Jockin!" said Barbara gently. "Nor used them ill. Think you, the good sisters asked to keep the baby and bring it up at the convent, and they do offer the mother employment there. If we had left it in the village as I wished, it had not been so blessed."

Philip demanded news of his monkey, Sir Richard wished for tidings of his wife. Edward wanted to hear from the jester's own lips every detail of their adventures.

They circled the new manor house, advising, planning, and settling where to plant Lady Isabel's garden and the new pear tree.

Then back through the forest to the Castle of Dean, bringing the happiness of reunion to cheer the months that must pass before their home was ready. And when Edward had returned to earn his knighthood in his uncle's house, with Philip accompanying him to follow in his footsteps, and Lady Barbara had returned to her aunt's side to begin her education in the convent, they would leave behind that part of the household that was always home to them, wherever it might be: their father, their mother, their younger sisters, and their jester, who would follow the family fortunes as long as he had breath to tell a story or to be kind to little children.